BOOK ONE OF THE REVELATION TRILOGY

Sword of The Angels

Matt Eastwood

Printed in Australia
First Printing, 2017
ISBN: 978-0-6480806-9-5
White Light Publishing House
Taylors Lakes, VIC, Australia 3038
www.whitelightpublishing.com.au

For Tim

Acknowledgements

My family has always supported me in everything I've ever done, and even though we've sometimes had our differences, we've always stuck together. After the loss of my brother, I learnt to appreciate my family a lot more than I already did. They were always my rock to stand on. Dad once told me, "you can choose your friends", meaning you can't choose your family. Well, Dad, if I did have the choice, I'd choose you guys every time. So, thank you, to Mum, Dad, Daniel, Mandi, Andrew and Tim. For everything.

I also wouldn't be where I am today, were it not for the brothers I have gained over the years. True friendship is hard to find, and I am so lucky to have these friends that I can call brother. The ones that despite arguments, still hung around. So, thank you to Luke Miller; you've always been a reassuring voice. Whether you agreed with me or not, you always listened. To Grant Heath; this book would be nothing without you. The countless hours spent in discussion about it, and the advice you gave is what made this story what it is today. And, to Shane Crosling; you've always been straight up with me, and everything you've done for me - whether it hurt me or not - you did for me because of how much you care. Having lost a brother, gaining brothers such as these has immensely changed my life.

The Revelation

The great sword was removed from battle for a greater purpose. When the time comes, the angel to which the sword is bound will have to search for his sword and reclaim it. Once he has reclaimed his sword, he will then assume the position he was chosen to fulfill, and a great alliance will be formed.

The angel will fall, and rise again with the great power that he was destined to behold. The most powerful sword must belong to the most powerful angel. The sword will strike the great stone and all the lost angels will rise up into the sky, and then the angel will reunite Heaven with its lost souls and begin the battle to fight for the good of the Heavens and the Earth.

To which an angel will be born of human blood and live as a human until the angel inside of him is set free. His identity will be found by the colour of his wings, for he will be a Seraph. The human angel will lead the armies of Heaven to victory. The sword will spill human blood and merge the two pieces, which will then harm its possessor, leading us to defeat the bringer of all evil. This revelation will be confirmed by the one true God.

CHAPTER I

"I'm gonna need another drink," he said almost as if to himself, as he took the last sip of scotch from his glass, "and leave the bottle."

Marcus was sitting in a small, almost saloon-like nightclub, that was dimly lit, with some top forty dance-type music playing over the large speakers, hanging from the roof in the corners of the dance floor. The DJ to his left had his headphones on one ear, and was listening to the next track he was about to play. The bartender looked over his shoulder at the small, slightly built figure at the end of the bar. "Marcus," he shouted over the music, "don't you think you've had enough for tonight?"

"I've only had one bottle."

The bartender noticed that he was quite coherent after an hour and a whole bottle of scotch, and wiped his forehead. "You've been coming in here pretty much every day for the past five years, and you drink all this scotch. This stuff must be preserving you, you look like you haven't aged a bit!"

"Just pour the drink." The bartender shrugged and opened another bottle. He poured him another drink and left the bottle right next to the glass with the lid off. "You're not causing any trouble, anyway." He backed away slowly with his hands up in the air, like there was nothing more that he could do.

Marcus closed his eyes and took a sip of his fresh drink, from a glass that looked like it had been through the glass washer a thousand times. He glanced left to the half-full dance floor to where his friend Ben was dancing with a young woman. She looked to be in her early twenties, but then again, so did Marcus. *Haven't aged a bit…* he thought, looking down at his glass. He half-smiled to himself and looked back over at Ben. Three large men approached him, moving with great hostility. One of the men pushed Ben and pointed a finger at the girl. "You dancing with my girl?" he said. Ben looked up at the man and tried not to look away from his intimidating stare. It's the first rule of staring; the first one to look away, loses. "Did you hear me?" Ben took a deep breath.

"Oh, I heard you, but I don't recall anybody telling me this is *your* girl."

"I'm not your girl," the young woman scowled.

"So, by the look of things, she can dance with whoever she likes."

The man's face quickly turned a deep shade of red. Ben fought off a quiver of his bottom lip while he kept eye contact with the man. After all, he was only human. He could handle this situation, but he knew somebody was there to back him up if need be; someone he trusted his life with, no matter how much they'd had to drink. Marcus sat at the bar and stared at the group on the dance floor, watching their every move like a hunter stalks his prey. He kept his eyes on the dance floor and pushed the bottle of scotch towards the bartender who was standing in front of him, wiping a glass. The bartender sensed something was wrong and looked at Marcus, who was already slowly on the move. Marcus sidestepped towards the end of the bar, never shifting his gaze. He sat on the bar stool closest to the dance floor, which was almost within arm's reach of Ben's tormentors. He sat, he waited, and he listened. "Maybe," the man barked, "but you won't be able to dance with *anybody* after this."

The man lunged forward with a left fist coming fast. The world around Ben started to move very slowly. He stood completely still. The man's fist was stopped abruptly by something soft, but firm; almost like punching an old mattress. The man looked down to see a young man in his early twenties with longish curly brown hair; his left palm wrapped tightly around his fist. "I think you've had enough," Marcus said.

The man tried to free his hand, but couldn't remove it from Marcus' grasp. Marcus looked him in the eye and tightened his grip. He pushed down on his fist and lowered it towards the ground. He tightened his grip the lower it went, and bent the man's wrist. The man crouched in pain. Marcus let go of his hand. "Come on Ben, let's go." Marcus and Ben turned around to walk away. As soon as their backs were turned, the man jumped at Marcus, using all his weight as his weapon.

Marcus turned quickly and wrapped his left hand around the man's throat, using his momentum to hoist him up in the air. The man struggled with his feet to try and get a grip on the floor. Marcus held him higher, pulled his right hand out from behind him and Ben noticed the flash of silver in Marcus' hand. "Marcus, NO!" he screamed.

Marcus held his dagger up to the man's throat. His eyes were burning through the man like fire, full of anger. He let out a quick burst of air, and dropped the man on the ground. He put the dagger behind his back. "Marcus, you'd better leave," the bartender said from behind the bar. The music sounded like a dull pulse in the background. The men picked up their friend from the dance floor and stared. Marcus felt all the eyes in the room on the back of his neck. He walked over to the bar and picked up his glass in one hand, and his jacket in the other. He gulped down the last mouthful of his drink and set the glass softly on the bar. "That's a nice drop," he said calmly as he pulled out his wallet and threw a hundred-dollar bill on the bar, "thanks Mike." He picked up the bottle of scotch and turned to walk out the door. Ben reluctantly followed.

The large "Murphy's" sign above the entrance to the bar lit up the tops of their heads. They turned left and started to walk east. "What the hell was that?" Ben asked. "What?"

"In there! That was incredible! That was weird! That was... not human. What was that?"

Ben looked at Marcus like he was from another planet. "That guy probably weighed two hundred pounds, and you just lifted him up in the air! And you held that dagger to his throat!" Marcus pulled out his dagger. He looked at it like a child looks at an old teddy bear. It was about fourteen inches long, with a Celtic pattern on both flats of the blade. Towards the handle, the blade barbed out in a wave of spikes. It was obviously designed to do more damage on the way out rather than the way in. "My trusty blade," he sighed. He put it away. They continued to walk east down the street, not uttering a word. Ben decided to break the silence. "I mean, you've taught me everything you know about fighting. I've never seen you do *anything* like that! That's like ninja stuff! Mind over matter, right?" Marcus took a drink from the bottle of scotch he'd taken from the bar. "No," Marcus replied. "It's something else."

"Right," said Ben awkwardly, "that was creepy!" They stopped at the next intersection to head their separate ways. "Okay, I'll see you tomorrow," Ben called out as he walked away backwards, turning around just after the last sound left his mouth. "Bye," Marcus said as he kept walking. He turned left onto a main road and walked north. He got to the front door of his apartment building, put the key in the door, and walked inside. He went up the elevator to the third floor and into a brown door with the number 23 on it; his apartment.

The morning sun shone through the window and Marcus slowly woke, as he sat up in bed. He threw his legs over the edge of the bed and planted his feet on the floor among the empty bottles. Obviously hung over, he sat there rubbing his eyes, trying to ignore the throbbing headache that was thumping like the music from the night before. He lit a cigarette and breathed out the toxic fumes. A glowing blue haze, like a strong blue light shining through fog started rising out of his back. The smoky haze began to form sharp points and grow even larger. It was an aura, but to many it would be known as wings. Marcus had seen depictions of angels before, with feathered wings. He used to comment and make jokes, "Because feathers are so angelic". He looked up at his wings floating in the air above him, slowly swaying almost like he was underwater, or trees in a soft breeze. Marcus stood up and butted out his cigarette in the ashtray, and walked into the bathroom to have a shower, with the hope of shaking off his still drunken state. He had the water on high, and at the hottest temperature. His wings rose up out of the shower stall and filled the entire bathroom. He took a long hard deep breath. "What am I doing?"

Marcus turned the shower off and dried himself, as his wings shrank back into his shoulder blades until they were completely hidden. As he got dressed, he sensed something wasn't right. He threw on his jacket and pulled the hood out from the sweat shirt he was wearing underneath. He walked through the small hallway entrance that led to his front door. There were wooden crosses on the wall on both sides of the hallway, and a large brown painted one on the ceiling above him. He walked across the rug that was taking up the entire entrance hallway and opened the front door of his apartment. There he saw three men; all with very similar faces, and long black coats standing in the door way. "Hello Marcus," they all said. They spoke together in unison, but it was only one voice. Marcus knew exactly who they were. *He* was walking the earth, and he was walking in three. Marcus quickly slammed the door in their faces and ran for the window. He dove through head first, shattering the glass, and fell three stories down to the sidewalk below. The concrete cracked under his black and chrome boots, as he landed on his feet. Shards of glass bounced and scattered on the ground around him. He looked left and right. People all around him stared at him in disbelief. Before they could ask if he was okay, he began running south. He didn't want to believe he saw the three men, because he knew exactly why they were there.

It's started, he thought, as he ran.

Ben opened his front door to see Marcus standing there, a little out of breath. He looked Marcus up and down and knew something was up. He hadn't seen him so unhinged before. He was looking over his shoulder as if somebody was following him. "Something chasing you?" he asked.

"No, why do you ask?" Marcus replied as he lit a cigarette.
"Well you're out of breath, and smoking doesn't help that by the way. And, you keep looking over your shoulder. Everything okay?"

"Let's just say I ran into some people I didn't particularly want to see again."

"I hope it wasn't our friends from last night."

"No, much worse than that."

"What could possibly be worse than three guys that probably want to kill you?" Ben asked in disbelief.

"That's pretty much what I came across."

Ben looked sideways at Marcus. "You mean there is more than one group of people that want to kill you?"

"Let's just say I've lost count."

Ben opened his eyes wide. He sat on the edge of his couch and ran his fingers through his hair, wondering why Marcus hadn't discussed this sort of thing with him before. "Like who?" he asked. "You wouldn't understand. It was all before I met you."

"You see?" Ben said, "All these things you say I wouldn't understand about things that happened before I met you. You keep half-mentioning things. I think some of that came out last night when you held your dagger to that guy's throat. What happened in your past that makes it so damn special to keep hidden?"

Marcus was quick to respond. "Speaking of which, why did you back down last night? I taught you better than that. You could have easily taken that guy. He was just muscle, you've got the brains!"

"Yes, but I was with that girl," Ben said in defence, "and I didn't want her to think I was a fighter. She told me about all her ex-boyfriends being fighters, and she hated it! I didn't want to come across as the same type of guy she'd been with before. Stop changing the subject!"

Marcus took a deep breath. "I can't tell you right now. But I will someday."

"Whatever!" Ben said to drop the conversation. "What do you want to do today?"

"Let's go see what Ryan is up to."

They left the house and Ben locked the door behind them. He slid his keys into his pocket as they started walking down the street. Their friend Ryan Harrison was just slightly older than Ben, and he had a wife and a young boy, named Julian, but everyone just called him Jules. Ryan was a black-belt in jujitsu and kyokoshin, and was probably one of the nicest martial artists you'd ever meet. He and Marcus taught Ben everything, from hand to hand combat, to weapons. Ben favoured the bow staff, whereas Marcus was a swordsman. Ryan was adept at both, but they all knew that Ben was better with the staff, and Marcus with the sword. Ryan knew what Marcus was, as Marcus had told him. He could tell him just about anything, and he was trustworthy, so he kept the knowledge to himself. He even kept it from Ben, as he knew Marcus didn't like divulging that information, and he understood that the less people that knew, the better. However, if Ben were to ever ask, Ryan was always funny about lying to people. So, he hoped the situation never arose.

They approached his door and Marcus knocked subtly. They heard the footsteps echo on the floorboards as Ryan walked to the door. He opened up with a smile and stepped forward to shake both of their hands. He was around thirty, with arms hairier than a grizzly bear, and a beard that was probably shaven that morning, but had grown almost a few millimetres in mere hours. His hair was about the same length as his stubble and was slightly receded, with a real salt and pepper colour about it. His clothes were two sizes too large for him. He cracked a slight smile. "How are we fellas? Come in! Come in!" He turned to walk inside as they followed. "You're just in time too! I was about to head down to the dojo to teach. I'd love for you to join me. You could probably help me knock some sense into these arrogant little pricks." Marcus grinned. "Do you really want me to do that, Ryan?"

Ryan turned and returned Marcus' grin. "Maybe not you. I'd rather I didn't have to call the morgue." Ben half forced a grin. He knew Marcus was good, and had a temper, but he never saw him as any better than himself. He always thought they were pretty evenly matched, even though Marcus trained Ben from scratch. "I'm off to the dojo, honey," Ryan called out to his wife, "I'll see you later!" They all hopped into Ryan's car and headed for the dojo.

"Any interesting students?" Ben asked. Ryan smiled. "One in particular. An arrogant little shit. Goes by the name of James McIntyre. I'll admit, he's good, but cocky. I gotta teach him a lesson, let him know he's not as good as he thinks he is." Marcus looked out the window. "I'll put the fear of God in him", he said. They arrived and Ryan parked the car against the curb and got out. Ryan lead up the staircase to a door with writing on it. *Ryan Harrison, Elite Training.* It opened up into a long corridor with a door on either side, and a glass window in the top half of both doors. Ryan walked into the one on the right, as Ben and Marcus followed. "Alright, folks," Ryan said. The room had close to twenty people standing in it; stretching, preparing, and waiting for Ryan's arrival. "This is Ben and Marcus, they'll be observing today. They are as well trained as myself and may step in from time to time, so please show them the respect you would show me. They are faster, stronger, and much, much smarter than you. So please, don't mess with them."

Marcus took a seat near the door and sat to watch as Ben stood next to him and leaned against the wall. He rested his hand on a table just next to him, and noticed a balanced throwing knife lying on the table. He picked it up and rested it point down on the table as he slowly spun it around. They both watched Ryan address the class and begin showing certain techniques, then had the class repeat them with partners. Ryan kept a close eye on one in particular. He moved over to the table and took a drink from his water bottle, and caught Ben's' eye. "That the troublemaker? The one you keep looking at?" Ben asked. Ryan looked over at young James McIntyre. "That's the one."

Ryan went back and continued to work with them as Ben cautiously watched James McIntyre. He was around the same age as Ben, maybe slightly younger, with jaw length brown hair, and a very arrogant look on his face. To his credit, he was *very* good. He had excellent technique for a young man, but Ben noticed he was very cocky about it. Ben took the knife in his hand and swapped it to his right hand, as he flipped it around and held it by the blade. He watched on. James McIntyre was sparring with a young woman in her early twenties. She was a yellow belt, which meant low contact, since she was still learning. Ben saw it in James' eyes before he saw the movement. James stepped forward with his left leg and came a little too close with a prepped right leg. Ben stepped off the wall and flung his right arm back, quickly jerking it all the way forward and releasing the throwing knife. It hurtled through the air, spinning around madly as it edged closer and closer to James' head. The class had stopped and all eyes were on the knife as it spun and spun across the room at full speed. Time felt like it had slowed down as it seemed to take forever to make the journey across the room, and James was the last one to see it. His peripheries saw something flying towards him as he was bringing his right leg up for a full contact roundhouse kick, as he turned his head and saw the knife almost upon him. He bailed from the kick and fell backwards as fast as he could, in great fear. The knife passed just in front of his face and embedded itself into the wall behind him. James fell hard and fumbled a little as he stepped back to his feet.

All eyes were on Marcus and Ben, as Marcus slightly shifted his chair a few inches away from Ben and looked away as he discreetly pointed up at Ben and pretended to cough, trying to act nonchalant. Ben stared furiously at James who was regaining his composure. "Who threw that?" James shouted. The room was silent. "I did", Ben said. James squared his eyes on Ben for a moment, contemplating what to do or say next.

"You're lucky I saw that and moved out of the way in time!" Marcus stood up. "No, you're lucky. Had you not moved, you'd be dead." Marcus looked at Ben. "I probably would have stopped it differently, but hey, that works too", he said as he moved away.

Ben walked over to James. "Yellow belt," Ben said, "means low, to no contact. You were six inches too close as you prepped your roundhouse, and from the angle of the wind up, you were aiming for her head. She's not trained enough to block such a blow. You could have done some serious damage." Ryan looked over at James who was looking down and shifting his eyes around to remember his positioning, and trying to come up with an excuse. "I was gonna pull it. I wouldn't have hit her, you psycho." Marcus walked over to James, quietly, slowly and confidently, with no expression on his face. Once he was right next to him, he leaned into his ear. "I saw it too," he whispered, "and if I see you disrespect this *art* again, you'll wish the knife *had* hit you." Marcus held a long stare as James shrunk under it. He slightly gulped and nodded. "Carry on," Marcus said. Marcus walked over to his chair and sat down again as Ryan beckoned the class to continue. He stood next to Ben watching his students, as he leaned over slightly. "And I thought Marcus was bad. You're as bad as he is."

Ben and Marcus left the dojo and walked down the dark secluded street, heading towards Murphy's, content in quiet conversation between them, about nothing entirely particular. They eventually got around to talking about the night before.

"I hope those guys aren't there tonight," Ben said. "So, what if they are?" Marcus replied, "It's not like they're gonna be able to do anything."

"No, it's just that I hope that girl from last night is there. She was great! I really liked her, and I was hoping to get to know her better." At that moment, as they approached the door to Murphy's, the three men from the night before lurked out of the alley way between Murphy's and the take away restaurant next door. They walked up behind Marcus and Ben with an almost rehearsed stride. "So, you're still interested?" one of them asked. Ben and Marcus both turned around to see the three men standing there. The man in the middle was obviously the ringleader, and was still holding a grudge about the night before. The sheer jealousy in his eyes made Ben look down instantly. Ben had lost the staring competition this time around. He looked back up at the man, and shrank under his stare as the man pulled a long sword out from behind his back. "Can I interest you in this?"
Ben anxiously stepped back, while Marcus stood completely still. The man waved the sword back and forth in front of the two with a sense of victory. "Yeah! Not so tough, *now* are you? Let's see how *you* go against a sword." The man focused his attention on Marcus. Marcus held his ground; didn't move, didn't avert his eyes. He just held the man's stare with a blasé look on his face. "Ben," Marcus said calmly, "run."

Ben turned around to see that they were surrounded. Obviously, the men had recruited others, in case the situation was out of their control. "Umm," Ben stuttered, "I can't. We're sort of surrounded!"

"No problem," Marcus mumbled. Marcus grabbed the back of Ben's' shirt and threw him one handed, in one single movement, onto the awning above the Murphy's entrance. The instigator swung the sword at Marcus who had already drawn his dagger. He held it with the blade reversed towards his elbow and blocked the man's blow. He kicked the man in the stomach, who then went stumbling backwards. The man fought to maintain his balance and stood with his legs apart, waiting for Marcus to start him. Marcus kicked the very tip of the sword, which sent shock waves down the blade to the handle in the man's hand. "How's your hand?" Marcus grinned. "That's the problem with knock offs. They don't handle shock very well." The man's hand started trembling uncontrollably. Marcus stepped closer to the man and kicked his hand. The man dropped the sword and clutched his palm with a small gasp. He bit his bottom lip. Marcus lunged into a forward step with his left leg, and in the same movement his right leg came towards the man with a ferocious force behind it. He planted his right heel into the man's sternum as the man went tumbling backwards. *Ring leader down,* Marcus thought to himself.

As Marcus took a second to assess who would run at him next, he noticed that their attention was already focused on something behind him. Before he could turn, the sword ripped through his stomach, like a whale leaps out of water. Marcus didn't even flinch. He looked down at the blade sticking out of his stomach, then realised why everybody had stood and waited. He looked up and rolled his eyes.

Ben struggled to look down from the awning, trying to see what was happening. He couldn't get a good view. He knew Marcus was in trouble, but had no idea what was happening, or what he could do to help. He couldn't help but wonder why Marcus had thrown him up onto the awning, or why Marcus was so fearless as to sacrifice himself to save him. Ben knew how to fight just as well as Marcus; they were a great team, and Ben never backed down from a fight, until tonight. Maybe that was why Marcus threw him up onto the awning. Ben stopped to think for a second. *How did Marcus throw me onto the awning? Somebody his size? That's not possible!* Ben came back to reality and tried to find a way down.

Marcus slowly turned around to see who had stabbed him. A very small and thin man stood in his shadow. For someone to look up at Marcus in fear, they would have to be quite small. Marcus was only about 5'10, and in situations like this, his opponent was usually looking down at him. Marcus grabbed the small man by the shirt, and forcefully pulled him forward, like an act of intimidation. The sword sticking out of Marcus' stomach punctured the man's chest with great force, and went straight through him. The small man let out a gasp. Marcus pushed him away and off the sword, and threw him on the ground. He reached behind him, pulled the sword out from his back, and threw it on the ground next to the small man. Marcus' wound started healing instantly. He turned to walk away. The rest of the men surrounding him rushed to their friend on the ground that was bleeding. Marcus stopped and slowly turned around. All the men crouching on the ground next to their friend were staring at Marcus. He had just killed out of anger.

Marcus started walking back towards the group of men, and pushed them out of the way. He cupped his hands together over the wound on the man's chest. A bright light started shining from underneath his palms, and the men tried to cover their eyes to avoid being blinded, but they didn't want to miss what was going on in front of them. The man's wound healed as he sat up and coughed up the remaining blood from the injury. Marcus stood up, and the men all stared in awe. In turn, they looked up at Marcus. The man from the night before stood up and looked down at Marcus' stomach. "What are you?" He asked. Marcus looked at the small man recovering, dazed on the floor, and then up at the man standing in front of him. "You wouldn't believe me if I told you."

Marcus turned around and walked away. Ben eventually found his way down from the awning and saw the group of men crouched on the ground. The man standing up pointed behind Ben to where Marcus was walking. Ben looked behind him, and turned back to the man. "Thank you," he said gracefully. Ben ran after Marcus. As he caught up with him, he looked at him in distrust. "What happened?"

"Don't worry about it. It's finished." Marcus didn't move his eyes. It was almost as if he was determined to get somewhere, but didn't know where. "Why did you throw me up on the awning?" Marcus stopped and breathed out heavily. He turned to look at Ben. "I didn't want to see you get hurt."

Ben relaxed his shoulders and stared at Marcus. "Didn't want me to get hurt? I'm pretty much just as good as you!"

"You hesitated."

"Yes, I did!" Ben snapped. "But I realised, and then I was ready to fight."

"You still could have been hurt." Marcus kept walking.

"Oh what," Ben chased after him, "and you can't? Why do you think you're so high and mighty that you can't be hurt? Even killed! You're not invincible you know?"

"Not that you know of," Marcus muttered under his breath.

"What?" Ben asked.

"Nothing."

"Whatever!" Ben scoffed, as he headed down his street. "I'll see you later." Ben stormed off. Marcus started walking the same way to his apartment building. As Ben got halfway to his house, he had the sudden urge to go and talk to Ryan about the situation he had just faced with Marcus. He turned around and began walking to Ryan's' house, hoping he'd be home and could talk. He made his way there and knocked on the door as Ryan's' wife answered the door. She looked at him with a smile. "Hi Ben, try to kill anyone else today?" Ben half smiled. "You heard about that, huh?" She stepped aside allowing him to walk in. "I'm sure a lot of people are going to hear about that one. Just don't get yourself into trouble, okay? I know deep down you have a good heart, and wouldn't harm anyone for no reason."

"Thanks Beth," Ben said. "that means a lot. Is Ryan back yet? Or did he tell you over the phone?"

"He's here, he's just getting out of the shower. I'll tell him you're here."

"Thank you."

Beth walked away as Ben sat down on the couch. He noticed young Julian playing over in the corner with some toy cars. He looked over and smiled at the young boy. He'd always wanted a son, but never actually settled down. He came close once, with a girl he used to date by the name of Alexandra. He thought of her briefly as Ryan walked into the room. "Ben!" he said, "no knives?" Ben laughed and stood up to shake Ryan's' hand. "Not on me, no. Is there uh... Somewhere we can talk?"

"Of course, my office."

Ryan walked towards a hallway in the back of the house that lead to a guest room, young Julian's room, and a bathroom. At the end of the hallway it opened up into a laundry with a sliding glass door, and out in the backyard was a small bungalow. It wasn't really an office. Just a man cave, of sorts. A bar in the corner, a desk with a basic computer, a couch and a television. Ryan walked over to the bar and opened a small fridge under the counter, pulling out a beer for himself and one for Ben. He held it up to offer it to Ben who took it without a sound. Ben sat down on the couch, wondering how to start the conversation, as his eyes darted back and forth.

Ryan watched him closely, figuring what he might say. "Marcus did something, didn't he?" Ryan asked.

Ben looked up. "How did you know?"

Ryan sat down next to Ben on the couch with a bottle opener and opened both his and Ben's' beers. He flicked both lids into a small bin in the corner and sat back. "I know that look," Ryan said. "He did something that you can't explain, and now you're wondering how, and what, and why, and thought that I might know something." Ben turned his head towards Ryan. "Do you?" he asked.

"That all depends. What did he do?"

Ben took a deep breath and tried to remember every detail. He wanted another perspective, and he could always trust Ryan. "We were confronted by some guys that we had trouble with last night. They'd recruited more guys and surrounded us. Marcus threw me up on the awning above Murphy's' entrance. One handed." Ryan half smiled. "Yeah, he has the strength of a dozen elephants, doesn't he?"

"Ryan, one handed! He and I weigh about the same. How is that even possible? And, last night, he picked the guy up and held him off the ground one handed. The guy was huge!"

Ryan straightened up and got a serious look in his eye. "Ben, with Marcus, you've seen what he's like. Self-sacrificing, tempered, and probably one of the best fighters I've ever seen."

"I'm just as good as he is!" Ben shouted.

Ryan shook his head. "You're great, Ben. But, I guarantee you, Marcus would have one up on you. Sorry bud, no disrespect, but he's just something else, man. They broke the mould when they made him."

Ben shook his head. "I don't understand. I know he's a great fighter, and I've seen him take on multiple opponents, whilst drunk, and come out unscathed, but he's still human. He just has no regard for his own safety."

"How many?" Ryan asked.

"How many what?"

"How many have you seen him take on at once?"

Ben thought for a second. "Well I didn't really see anything tonight, so the most is three, the day I met him. He annihilated them!"

"Seven," Ryan said. "Seen him take on seven."

Ben opened his eyes wide. "Seven guys? At once? Surely they were common thugs with no skill or technique."

"Gang affiliated, knives and guns, dude. One even got a shot off. Marcus didn't have a scratch on him. He's blessed, man."

"Is that even true?"

"One hundred percent," Ryan said. "Hear what I'm saying. The dude's blessed."

"Blessed? I doubt it. I mean, I know he's a little religious and all, but blessed? Come on."

"A little religious, you're smart. You'll figure it out."

"You *do* know something!" Ben shouted.

"All I know, is that when Marcus is ready to tell you something, he'll tell you man. It's not up to me."

Ben sat silently, wondering what the secret could be.

* * *

"Let's just take it!" the man said. "He won't wake up."

Three men with shaved heads and long black coats were standing in Marcus' bedroom, eyeing off the sword in his half-closed hand. It wasn't the same three as before. Marcus had other methods of stopping demons getting into his apartment. He had hooked up the alarm system to the sprinklers, with which he had blessed the water from the tanks that they came from. If he wasn't home, the alarm would trigger the sprinklers and cover the demons in holy water. He didn't care much about human thieves. But, if the seal of crosses at the front door didn't work, the holy water would. This time, Marcus was at home.

"But, we want to make sure he *doesn't* wake up," another man said. "Remember what we were told: destroy the sword, you destroy him."

"What, you think this is the Sword of the Angels?" Marcus asked, as if talking in his sleep. He sat up in bed and looked at the three men. "Does this dagger even look close to a heavenly sword?" The three men instantly disappeared with a black cloudy substance evaporating quickly after them. Marcus put his head back on the pillow.

"What are you doing Marcus?" The voice filled the entire room, booming with a broad resonance. Marcus sat up and looked around. He didn't see anyone, but he recognised the voice.

"Eran. What do you want?" he asked as he slowly lay back down. A white mist started rising up out of the floor. It formed a human like shape, and then turned into an old man, dressed all in white. The man had a white beard, and a silver haze rose up out of his back and formed into wings the same as Marcus'. Marcus knew him well. Eran, a Throne; was one of the choirs of angels in the second sphere of the Hierarchy of Angels; more commonly known as Heavenly governors. Marcus himself, was a Cherub. The Cherubs were the second highest choir of angels in the first sphere; higher up the chain of command. The angel looked down at Marcus. "You mean you don't know? You've been here all this time, and when I come to see you, you ask what I want? You can't have had that much to drink that you've forgotten why you're here."

"I haven't forgotten." Marcus sleepily replied.

"Perhaps we can go somewhere safe to talk." Eran put his hand on Marcus' shoulder and they were suddenly in a church, with big arched stained-glass windows, and a tall roof. Eran glided over to the stage and hovered there with his silver wings flowing above him. Marcus was lying down over to the side. He picked himself up and leaned against the wall. "So, speak. Tell me what you came here to tell me." Eran looked at Marcus like he had told him a thousand times. "You know exactly what I came here to tell you. You're just too stubborn to listen."

"I know, I know. You want me to find the sword. That's why I've been here the past seven hundred years. I looked, and I never found it."

"So, you stopped looking? You do remember that you aren't allowed back into Heaven without it, don't you?"

"I'll find it."

"Not at this rate you won't," Eran remarked. "You've given up! It's not like you've been asked of much. After all, it is *your* sword. I figured you'd do anything to get your hands back on the most powerful sword in existence!"

"I said I'll find it." Marcus looked at the floor, almost as if a parent was telling him off.

"We even sent you help, and you haven't even attempted to try to use it."

"What help?" Marcus looked sideways at the angel. Eran motioned over to Ben, who was lying asleep on the floor. Marcus followed his gaze and saw Ben lying there. Eran had obviously transported him to the church as well. "No, not him! He doesn't need this. It's too much for him! How did he get here?" Marcus stared at Ben.

"It's why he was born; to help you," Eran said "His whole life has been leading up to this very moment, and there is no way you can do this without him."

"But, why him?" Marcus didn't want Ben to have to deal with the things he had been through. He knew that if Ben were to come along, it would change him. Eran glared at Marcus.

"He is the descendant of Amalie."

Marcus stared at Eran in shock. He couldn't believe what he had just heard. "You're joking, right?" he asked.

"Why would I? I'm not a comedian!"

"He's the bloodline? The one we... the one *I* have spent most of my life protecting, to the point I even hid them from myself? It's him? He's just a kid!"

Marcus looked back down at Ben, asleep in the middle of the floor. "Ben!" he called. Ben woke up and looked around. He was slightly disoriented and couldn't stop his eyes wandering. *Where am I?* he thought to himself. He looked over at Marcus, and then at the angel standing up by the altar. He pointed at Eran and opened his mouth to speak, but no sound came out. "Yes Ben, an angel," Marcus stated.

"You can see him too?"

"Ben," Eran said. "Marcus is an angel. Of course, he can see me."

Ben looked at Marcus. "No, he's not, he's a man. Just like me, aren't you?"

Marcus was staring at the floor. His eyes darted up at Ben who was now sitting upright on the floor. Marcus slowly shook his head. Ben stared at him with wide eyes. "No, it's not possible," he said, skeptically.

Eran nodded at Marcus, who looked away with malcontent. *I can't believe I'm doing this,* he thought. He stood upright and in a large flash of blue, his wings appeared instantly. They swayed and danced above his head, filling the room with a blue glow. Ben stared in awe. At that moment, a priest walked through the archway and into the church hall. He looked up at the two angels in disbelief. He stopped for a second and dropped his jaw. He fell to his knees and threw his arms up in the air.

"Oh, Heavenly angels!" he screamed, "Please bless this House of God."

Marcus looked at the priest kneeling on the floor. The priest quivered with fear, but also excitement. Marcus walked over to him. "This house is already blessed. That's why we're here. Please, go back to your chambers, and don't mention this to *anybody*. Even believers can be skeptical." The priest nodded. He turned around and walked out through the archway. Marcus turned back to Eran and Ben.

"So, where were we?"

Ben looked at Marcus in horror. "You're an angel!" he said, "You have wings. Now I understand what Ryan meant by blessed."

"Ryan?"

"Yeah, he just said you're blessed. I didn't get it. Now, I guess I do."

"Does that help you with my past?" Ben nodded silently. They both turned to Eran, and Ben sat on the floor again.

"Ben," Eran said, "You were born to aide Marcus in his quest. You see, he was supposed to come to earth to claim back his sword. The Sword of the Angels."

"Why is it on earth?" Ben asked.
"It was put here for a greater purpose." the angel said.

"What greater purpose would it have here? Wouldn't it be far more useful in the hands of an angel?" Marcus smirked.

"Wait, is that the sword that is guarding the entrance to the Garden of Eden?"

Marcus looked at Ben with great realisation. He half-leaped, half-glided over to the bible on the lectern. He opened it and flicked through it to Genesis 3:24. "So he drove out the man; and he placed at the east of the Garden of Eden Cherubs, and a flaming sword which turned every way, to keep the way of the tree of life," he read. He looked down at Ben. "Clever boy! he said.

"You see? You've been here for seven hundred years and you haven't even figured *that* out yet! You need him!"

Ben looked up at Marcus. "You've been here for seven hundred years?" Ben asked.

"Give or take a few," Marcus replied.

"What have you been doing all this time?" Ben looked at Eran, and then back at Marcus. There was a cool draft flowing through the room, and the deafening silence was only interrupted by the wind battering against the outside walls. Marcus breathed a deep breath. "I'll tell you later," he said.
"No!" Ben shouted, "You'll tell me now! You're not putting this one off." Marcus sighed. He looked at Eran, then up at the roof.

"The first hundred years, I searched. And, I wasn't going to give up. I made that sword. It belonged to me, and it was taken away from me."

"It was far too powerful. That's why it needed a greater purpose," Eran remarked.

Ben looked puzzled. He didn't know if he had heard right or not. "You made the sword?"

"Yes," Marcus replied.

"How?" Ben questioned.

Eran cut in to answer Ben. "Ben, Marcus is the Commander of Battle in the armies of Heaven. When a Commander of Battle retires his position, he then chooses another angel to take his place. Before Marcus, there was Arus; a fierce warrior. All feared and respected him. He chose Marcus to take over, long before he retired. Archangels are usually selected to take the position, and Marcus was an Archangel at the time. Marcus then made the Sword of the Angels from the fires of hell."

"The fires of hell? Wouldn't that make it evil?" Ben asked.

"Depends on the angel. But it would also make it powerful. When the sword is made, it is bound to the angel. The more powerful the angel, or the more powerful the angel would become, the more powerful the sword. This particular sword was *too* powerful. Whilst Marcus was still young, it could corrupt him, or even kill him. So, it was taken off him to guard the entrance to paradise. Seven hundred years ago, Arus was forced to retire, and Marcus was asked to find his sword to take up his position."

"Why was Arus forced to retire?"

"Because he fell in love," Marcus said, "with a human."

"Why is that so bad?" Ben asked.

"Because we're here to serve, not to perve!"

"Marcus!" Eran scowled. "Highly uncalled for."

"Hey, it's true!" Marcus smirked.

"Anyhow," Eran continued, "the past seven hundred years, he's been on earth, supposedly trying to find his sword; with no luck."

"Hey!" Marcus shouted, "I know where it is now, don't I?"

"With some assistance."
"The only thing I don't know is how to get there." Marcus looked defeated; like he still didn't know where it was. Eran moved closer to him. He looked Marcus in the eye. "You know someone who does. In fact, someone very close to you knows." Marcus looked sideways at Eran. His mind raced through everyone that he knew. It finally came to him. "Lucifer," he said.

"Lucifer?" Ben shouted. "The Devil?"

"No no, don't call him that. He *hates* it when people call him that," Marcus replied.

"You know what to do. And, you'll need to make more swords for this journey. We fear you will need them," Eran said. "And, don't forget. You can't take him straight to Hell. He's a human. You have to go the back way. We can't risk losing him."

"Why's that?" Ben asked.

"Because those who enter Hell naturally, fall. We can't allow you to go that way, because we need you," Eran said.

CHAPTER II

After Eran left, Marcus and Ben went back to Ben's house so that he could get dressed. He threw on his jeans and his hooded sweat shirt, and fiddled with his short black hair in the mirror. Marcus walked into the bathroom. "Are you ready to go?" he asked.

"As ready as I'll ever be," Ben replied.

They were instantly standing in a national park next to a large stone tower sticking out of the ground. The tower was flat on all sides, and looked like something had tried to climb up it from each side, but fell and left large claw marks down the sides. The cliff was tall and had a hollow in it that looked like it had an archway carved into it. But there were no doors; just a rocky cliff face. "Come on," Marcus said.

"Where are we?" Ben asked.

"Wyoming," Marcus said as he pointed to the bushland around them. Ben looked around, and then looked back at the cliff. "Wyoming? And, what is this cliff?" Ben asked.

"Devils Tower. It's kind of like the tuning fork of the earth. In the Revelation, it speaks of the sword striking the great stone and all the angels living here on earth will rise up into the sky, and unite against the armies of evil," Marcus said, like he'd read the Revelation a million times.

"The Revelation?"

"It's kind of like a prophecy," Marcus said. "It's why I'm here. The sword it speaks of, is the Sword of the Angels. The most powerful sword in existence. Or, so I'm told."

"What have I gotten myself into?" Ben quietly asked himself.

Marcus looked up at the archway hesitantly. He walked straight through the cliff face under the arch. As he walked through the wall, flames appeared around his body, and then evaporated. Ben watched as the wall turned back to normal. Ben walked up to the wall, not wanting to pass through it. *On the other side of this wall is Hell!* he thought. All of a sudden, Marcus' hand appeared back through the wall of the cliff face. He knew it was Marcus' hand by the large silver ring on his thumb. The hand beckoned Ben to come through the wall. Ben hesitated as Marcus' hand grabbed him by the arm. He disappeared through the wall in a burst of flames. "There! That wasn't so bad, was it?" Marcus asked as Ben crashed through into Hell.

They were in a stairwell, made of stone. There were torches aflame on the walls leading down the stairs, that gave the rock colour an eerie red tint. Marcus began descending as Ben reluctantly followed, whilst each step grew wider, the further down they went. The stairwell opened out at the bottom and they set foot on the ground, as Ben let his eyes adjust to the sight around him. "This is Hell?" he asked, looking around. They were standing on a mountain, and below was a modernised society with tall buildings; practically completely on fire. He looked down and was mesmerised by the idea that it looked like a large city below them. He could see far into the distance, beyond the city. Flames erupted like great explosions all around, as the whole view in front of him glowed a bright crimson. There were bodies everywhere; either corpses on the ground, or masses fighting each other. Many looked human, but Ben saw creatures that could only be a thing of nightmares. Demons roamed unchallenged, chasing after what Ben figured were the damned. They were red skinned, but it was almost a grey-red. Even though Marcus and Ben were at a distance, Ben could make out the closest ones. Their skin was scaly, and they had big black menacing eyes. They too, had wings, but they seemed superfluous to what else Ben could see. People were falling from the red clouded sky above them; not to their deaths, it would seem, as Eran had said that those who enter Hell naturally, fall. It was as if the damned had no chance.

Demons and other creatures were upon them in seconds. It was mayhem. Winged creatures roamed the sky, and Ben squinted to try make out their shape. They looked worse than the demons on the ground; and bigger. Ben stepped up next to Marcus, looking out at the sight. It looked like a rundown city with decayed bodies all over the ground, and explosions erupting everywhere.

"It looks just like Manhattan!" Ben said.

"It pretty much is. Only *everybody* here is a drug dealer, a murderer, or a thief," Marcus replied. "By the way, watch your pockets." Ben looked down at his pockets and quickly put his hands in them. In the far distance, there was a house in the middle of what looked like fields, that ran for miles and miles. It was the only thing that didn't look red. It was pure white, and untouched by the constant flames that seemed to plague the rest of Hell. They began walking down a path that lead down the mountain. "Walk in front of me," Marcus instructed, "I can protect you from behind."

"But who's gonna protect me from the front?"

"They won't come at you from the front, if I'm behind you."

"And why is that?" Ben asked.

At that moment, a demon landed right in front of Ben. Its wings were like bat wings, and large, with the same reddish grey tint to them. It had big eyes and large teeth, and began to snarl at Ben. Marcus drew his dagger. "Back off!" he said, "He's with me." The demon saw Marcus and recognised him instantly, and flew away.

Marcus and Ben walked further down the mountain and into the city. Ben was scared, seeing the scenery in front of him. The streets were flooded with people and demons, and the sights were horrifying, as people were torn limb from limb. Ben fought off the urge to vomit, with a small shiver down his spine. Marcus opened up his blue wings, put his hand on Ben's shoulder and began leading Ben. As they got closer, the crowd suddenly paid them attention and began to part, making a pathway for them to pass. Ben was terrified at how close he was to these creatures that had such a thirst for human flesh. They looked hungry, or thirsty, and Ben knew it could only be one thing, blood-lust. Nonetheless, they continued to part, letting Ben and Marcus walk through, and Ben felt more and more like a human shield. "You sure you're not just using me as a shield?" he asked.

"Have they attacked you yet?" Ben shook his head slowly.

"They really are afraid of you, aren't they?" Marcus didn't reply. He just kept walking with a hold of Ben's shoulder. Some of the winged beasts that were patrolling the skies began to land on rooftops and look down, but even they kept their distance. Ben looked up to see them perched, and noticed they looked like depictions he had seen of the devil. Large red muscular bodies, with horns protruding out of their heads and down their backs, in between two large red wings. Ben's fear grew more intense as he looked at them all, staring back at him with the same look in their eyes. He wondered whether they were as afraid of Marcus as the demons on the ground. They didn't seem to move, so he felt a little better. He couldn't take his eyes off of them, though.

"They're devils." Marcus said, "Yes, there is more than one, and no, they're not as powerful as *the* devil, but yes, they are very dangerous." Ben nodded, keeping his eyes on one in particular. The crowd behind them continued the slaughter they were immersed in before the disturbance of Marcus and Ben, as the crowd in front continued to part and make way.

They were close to the other side of the city and the devils on the rooftop all took off in flight to continue patrolling. They reached the edge of the city and Ben saw that the fields that ran for miles and miles were something else entirely. It was a wasteland in front of him, slightly down the hill. It was amassed with corpses and human remains, stacked at least one-story high. It was basically one large mass of human bodies and body parts that slightly resembled a gruesome, yet blooming array of cornfields. There were creatures all on top of the large mass, eating all the remains in front of them. It went on for miles in almost all directions, and there were thousands upon thousands of these creatures. They almost resembled dogs, but looked much worse. Their skin was a reddish brown, and scaly, like the demons. They were almost as big as a pony, with huge muscular shoulders and legs, and jaws that looked like they could bite through an engine block.

There was a path straight down the middle, that Ben finally realised was the direction they were heading. He began to feel faint, as his legs felt like jelly. "Don't you pass out on me now," Marcus said. Ben fought to gain his balance. He stood upright and stopped. The path ahead was wide, but there were still some remains strewn across it; a small enough amount to step over. Ben turned back and wrapped his arms around Marcus. "Can you please just fly me over this?" Marcus nodded and wrapped his arms around Ben, and took off in flight. Ben hugged closely into his chest as they flew over the miles and miles of corpses and hell hounds. The white house was right in the middle, and Ben hesitantly took a glance below. They landed on the ground right at the front of the house, and walked up to the front door as Marcus banged on it with the side of his fist three times. Ben turned to Marcus. "Why did you make me walk through all of that? Why didn't you just fly me over all of it from the entrance?"

Marcus gave an apologetic look. "You needed to see that, up close."

Ben looked horrified. "Why?"

"To see that I can protect you." Ben gave an accepting, yet clearly discomforted nod. The door opened and they saw a large man wearing a suit. He was a wide man with broad shoulders, and his neck was wider than his shaved head.

"I'll tell him you're here, Marcus," the man said, as he turned and walked down the corridor. They slowly followed. Ben looked around the corridor as he walked down. There were three doors on each side, and one at the very end. The heavy-set man walked in the end door, and into a large room where Lucifer was sitting on a throne-like chair, atop three curved steps that half circled around it. There were two men standing either side of him; one was average height and broad; the other was tall and thin. "Your brother is here with a human," the large wide man said. Lucifer sat up straight. "Well, let him in," he said with a distinguished accent.
The room lit up with flames as Marcus and Ben walked in. "Cut the act," Marcus said. "You don't need to impress him." Lucifer looked at Marcus and Ben with an almost childlike expression. "Fine!" he said. He clicked his fingers as the flames disappeared. The room turned into a beautiful white room, with paintings on the walls, and flowers in vases on

small tables in each corner. "Okay," Ben said, "that was unexpected."

"I may be the Prince of Darkness, but I'm still a Prince, nonetheless."

"So, you're the Devil?" Ben asked. There was silence in the room. Everyone stared at Ben. He looked around at everyone in turn. Marcus had perched himself across a chair in the centre of the room. He was the only one not looking at Ben. "I told you he hates being called that," Marcus said as he looked up. Lucifer stood up out of his chair and walked down the steps surrounding his throne. He was about 6'2, and well built, but not huge like his doorman. "You know, there's quite a difference between the Devil, and the Fallen Angel. You see, the Devil is big and ugly. Do I look big and ugly to you?"

Ben looked up at Lucifer. He was actually very handsome, and walked with a certain presence. "No, you don't," Ben replied.

"Don't you forget that!" Lucifer said as he walked over to Marcus. "And to what do I owe the pleasure, dear brother?"

Marcus looked up at him with a glint in his eye. "I know where it is," he said.

"You know where *what* is?" Lucifer asked. He caught on as soon as he closed his mouth. "The sword?" Marcus nodded.

"Well, where is it?" he asked. "Show it to me."

"I don't have it yet. I just said I know where it is," Marcus remarked. "I just don't know how to get there."

"Well?"

"Well?" Marcus asked back. "Where is the one place on earth that I don't know how to get to, and that *you* do?"

Lucifer stood up. He slyly looked in Marcus' eyes. "It's not, is it? No, it can't be. Could it?"

"Yes, it is. And you're going to take us there."

"Like hell I will!" Lucifer shrieked.

"And that's exactly where you'll stay if you don't," Ben said.

Lucifer looked over at Ben. He slowly walked sideways towards him, speeding up with every step. "You think you're so clever, don't you? After all, you're only human."

"No, he isn't," Marcus said from his chair. "You should know that better than anyone. As soon as he set foot through that archway, he was no longer among the living."

Ben stepped back. "Whoa, wait a minute. You mean I'm..."

Lucifer cut him off. "Yes, I'm afraid so. You can't pass into Hell or Heaven without crossing over. Didn't you know that?"

Ben looked at Marcus. "It's true," Marcus said. "You're technically no longer a living human." Ben took a minute to come to terms with what he had just figured out.

Lucifer looked at Marcus. "Why would I want to help *him* anyway?" he asked, referring to God.

"The Revelation," Marcus answered.

Lucifer scoffed. "We get to make more swords," Marcus bargained. Lucifer looked up at him with hope in his eyes. "Really?" Marcus nodded.

"You mean one for me as well?" Marcus nodded again.

"Very well," Lucifer said. "But Azazel and Asmodeus come with us."

"If they must," Marcus replied.

"To the fire pits!" Lucifer yelled.

He walked out the door and into the corridor. Followed by Marcus and Ben, and then Azazel, the short, wide man, and Asmodeus, the tall, skinny man. The five of them walked out the front door of the house, and walked around the back of the house towards the Flaming River. As they got to the edge, Lucifer opened up his gold wings and flew across it. Then, Azazel and Asmodeus opened up their wings. They looked like bats wings that had been charred from fire, and there was a black cloudy haze surrounding them. They both turned to look at Marcus and Ben, and then took off after Lucifer.

"What are they?" Ben asked.

"They're fallen angels. Their evil and hatred has mutated them. Demon wings, altered skin colour, things like that. Now come on."

Marcus turned towards the Flaming River and opened up his blue wings. They cast a blue glow over the ground beneath them. "Wait!" Ben said, "I can't fly!" Marcus turned around and looked at Ben, then above him. Marcus half smiled. "That's a shame. You're waiting here then?"

Marcus took off in a flash of blue. Ben stood there on the bank of the Flaming River, wondering why Marcus left him there. The sea of corpses and the hell hounds were all behind him. He felt something touch his shoulder. His eyes opened wider than they ever had before. He was in real danger here. He was in Hell, and alone. He slowly turned to see what had touched his shoulder, and noticed a white glow just behind him. He turned around quickly, but saw nothing there. But in the corner of his eye, he saw the white glow behind him again. This time, he looked up. His white wings floated above him. He was in awe. *So that's what they meant. I'm no longer human... I'm an angel.* Ben had caught on. He still didn't understand how by going into Hell, he'd become an angel. He didn't want to stand there alone any more. He tried his wings and shot straight up. He twisted and turned in the air, trying to figure out how to fly straight. He felt great, but at the same time, wished he were learning to fly somewhere else. He caught up to Marcus, still trying to learn to fly. He was almost flying sideways when he caught up. Marcus looked at him and smiled. "You'll get it," he laughed.

They landed on the other side of the river. Marcus' big black and chrome boots indented the ground he landed on. "So glad you could join us," Lucifer said to both Marcus and Ben. The fire pits were just ahead of them. They walked up to a large stone sticking out of the ground, half surrounded by fire. The stone was about waist height and flat across the top, almost resembling a table. Lucifer walked over to a large pile of metal, and picked out two pieces. "These look good. Let's get to work." He put one on the ground next to the stone, and held the other one in the fire for a long time. He twisted it, making sure the flames heated the core as well as the surface. Once the piece of metal was red hot, he grabbed a large hammer from the ground, and placed the glowing metal on top of the stone. He started hammering the metal into shape. Every time he hit the stone, it made a loud 'ping' noise. "I thought that was a stone. It sounds like metal," Ben said.

"It's Hells' Anvil," Marcus said. "The combination of the stone, the hammer, the fire, and whoever is crafting it, is what creates the power, and the bond between the sword and its possessor."

"When do I get one?" Ben asked.

Lucifer put the piece of metal into a large hole. Steam hissed out of the hole, and almost sounded like terrified screams. It was loud, and Ben covered his ears. "What on earth is that?" he yelled over the noise.

"This isn't earth," Lucifer replied calmly. "They're lost souls that bind themselves to objects when their bodies can no longer hold them."

Lucifer kept crafting his sword. He put it back in the hole of water. It hissed loudly again, but not as loud as last time. It was just normal steam this time around. It was a time-consuming process. Eventually, Lucifer finished his sword. He held it upright and close to his face. It reflected the fire from the pits surrounding him, and it began to glow neon red. He swung it around, testing its mobility. He liked his work. "The Sword of Lucifer. Perfect," he said. He moved over to where Azazel and Asmodeus were standing. Marcus handed his dagger to Ben. He walked over to the stone and picked up the second piece of metal. He knew these two swords wouldn't be as good as the Sword of the Angels, since the Commander of Battle is allowed to scour the earth, Heaven, Hell, and Purgatory to find the perfect piece of steel. Marcus found a unique piece so that the sword could never be replicated. The piece he held in his hand was practically stainless steel compared to *his* sword. He held it in the fire until it glowed, then began to work the steel with the hammer. Lucifer walked over to Ben. He stood with Ben watching Marcus briefly, whose back was facing them. "So, how long have you known him?" Lucifer asked.

Ben looked up at Lucifer, and then back at Marcus. "About seven years now. Why do you ask?"

"Has he trained you?"

"Well, yeah. Why?"

"So, you must be pretty good then, right?"

Ben grew tired of Lucifer's questioning. "I guess. Why?"

"Well, Marcus trained you. You *do* know about his past, don't you?"

Ben's' ears pricked up. After all the times Marcus shrugged off one of Ben's' questions to do with his past, now he might actually hear some truth. *Can I trust Lucifer to tell the truth?* he thought.

"What about his past?" he quietly asked.

Lucifer gave a sinister smile. "He hasn't been searching for the sword this whole time."

"I already know that," Ben said, with far too much confidence.

"What about his title?" Lucifer looked up at Marcus to make sure he was still busy with his sword.

"Title?" Ben looked at Lucifer. "What title?"

"Well, we sometimes hold these tournaments. Combat. Angels versus demons. Marcus has never lost. In fact, he's won every single tournament since he started, six hundred years ago. He's unbeatable. It's all to do with his mentor. He always wanted to be just like him."

"Arus?" Ben asked.

"Yes, but Marcus doesn't see that he has become exactly the same; feared and loved by all. So, if he taught you, you must be pretty good."

"I'm not too bad. I'm also sober most of the time." Ben tried to lighten the mood.

"Well yes, the problems began when he started drinking excessively."
"Why? What happened?" Ben was fully turned towards Lucifer now.

"He let his guard down." Lucifer drew his sword as the last word left his lips. He raised it above his head and swung hard towards Ben, but Ben was quick. He already had Marcus' dagger in his hand and in front of his face to block. Below the knuckles, and running along his arm with the tip of the blade near his elbow. Lucifer's sword struck it hard. Ben didn't move an inch. Lucifer corrected and stood upright. "You are good," he said, "you're *very* good."

He twirled the sword and came at Ben from the right. Ben used the dagger to deflect the blows. They circled each other, Ben anticipating every move. He wasn't going to strike. *Who will Marcus back up?* he thought, *me or him?* They kept circling, as Lucifer kept trying to swing. Ben kept blocking. Lucifer grabbed Ben by the shirt and pushed him up against the nearest rocky wall. Ben grabbed Lucifer and held him up against the same wall. They were both pressed into the wall, their faces two inches apart, their swords grinding together.

Marcus looked at his finished sword and turned to see Ben and Lucifer with locked swords. He knew instantly who had started it. He threw his new sword at Lucifer. It passed directly in between their two bodies and pinned Lucifer's cloak to the wall. They both stared at Marcus in astonishment. "My sword is finished," he said. He walked up to them and pushed Ben aside. Marcus pulled his sword out of the wall and glared at Lucifer. "You two better play nice. We need him," Marcus whispered.

"And why is that?" Lucifer scoffed.

"He is the descendant of Amalie."

Lucifer looked at Ben, then back at Marcus. "No, he can't be," Lucifer said. "How do you know?"

"I got a visit from an old friend. He told me about it, and about how Ben is supposed to help with the Revelation." Marcus let go of Lucifer.

"Who?" he asked, just as he figured it out. "Oh no, not Mr. Fancy Pants, Look at me! I'm the Governor?" he asked in a Scottish accent. "And, you actually listened to his nonsense?"

"Hey!" Marcus shouted. "We know where the sword is now, don't we? If it wasn't for him, I wouldn't have even told Ben, and he's the one who figured it out for us!"

"You really have faith in this boy, don't you?"

Marcus looked up at Lucifer. "Yes. I do."

Lucifer looked over at Ben, who was dumbfounded by the sibling rivalry. Lucifer held out his hand. Ben shook it. "Apologies, old chap! Didn't mean any harm by it. Was just testing your skills!" he said, as he patted him on the shoulder.

"So, where to now?" Lucifer asked Marcus.

"We have to go to Heaven. But, you have to stay here. They won't let you back in.," Marcus said.

"And you think they won't stop you?" Lucifer asked.

"They can try."

Marcus and Ben left the fire pits and flew back over the Flaming River. Ben still struggled with his wings, but was getting the hang of it. They headed towards the exit in the cliff face as Ben spoke up. "One thing I don't get," he said.

"What's that?" Marcus asked.

"Well," he hesitated, "Azazel and Asmodeus, you said their evil and hatred mutated them, whereas Lucifer is still perfectly normal. Why is that?"

Marcus sighed. "Lucifer isn't full of evil and hatred, he's just pissed off! An angel scorned."

They got to the exit and both walked straight through it. Ben let out a sigh of relief to be back on earth. It was dark, and he could faintly see the countryside around them. He turned to look at Marcus. "Who was Amalie?" he asked.

Marcus slowly breathed out. "You weren't supposed to hear that. Are you sure you're ready for this?" Marcus asked him. "As ready as I'll ever be I guess."

Marcus frowned. "Amalie was the woman Arus fell in love with."

Ben opened his eyes wide. "You said I'm her descendant. But that would make me..."

Marcus interrupted him. "Yes, a direct descendant of Arus. Welcome to the family."

"Don't be so discreet. I now know he's your father."

"How could you possibly know that?" Marcus turned to look directly at Ben, waiting for an answer.

"Why else would Lucifer back down so fast when you told him? Because you don't kill your own blood. It finally made sense to me when you told me who Amalie was."

"You're too smart for your own good."

"And what's with the different coloured wings? They're not feathers like everyone thinks."

Marcus couldn't resist. "Oh yeah, because feathers are so angelic!" he chuckled to himself.

"You've said that so many times. Now I know why, and it's still not funny."

Marcus stopped laughing. "There are different choirs of angels. You can tell their class, by the colour of their wings."

"So, what are you?" Ben asked.

"I'm a Cherub."

"A Cherub? That's the second highest, isn't it?"

"Yes, second highest choir."

Ben looked down, trying to remember all the other choirs, and Marcus jumped in. "It goes Seraphim, Cherubim, Ophanim, Thrones, Dominions, Principalities, Powers, Archangels, and Angels."

"I knew there was a reason you told me all that, years ago. So, Cherubim are blue?" Ben asked.

"No, Cherubim are blue and red. Blue is a warrior, red is a scholar."

"So, what was that angel we saw in the church?"

"He was a Throne. They're sort of like governors. They keep order in Heaven."

"And I'm just an angel?"

"That's right. With your background of fighting, you will probably head down the warrior path and become an Archangel. Then after that, maybe a Power. Whereas if you were more of a book smarts guy, you might become a Principality next."

"So, it doesn't necessarily go in order?"

"No. In fact, it rarely does. I've seen some angels go from Throne to Archangel, purely because they switched from politics to battle."

"Right," Ben said, "so we're going to Heaven now?"

"Yep, we just gotta get up top."

Ben looked at the cliff face and moved his eyes upward to where the top was. "I can't even see the top. It's practically in the clouds! You want me to climb up there?" he asked.

"Not climb, you idiot." Marcus' wings seeped out of his back slowly. "You have to learn how to fly, and I'd prefer I didn't teach you in Hell. Out here, there's no one for miles, and you won't fall into a river of lava." Ben nodded and opened his wings. He shot up in the air about three metres. "No, stop!" Marcus shouted. "You have to imagine it and believe it. Control it with your mind. They do whatever you think. If you think of yourself flying slowly, you'll fly slowly. If you think you have to be at the top of that cliff quickly then you'll shoot up like a bullet. Think slowly."

Ben relaxed his wings. He started slowly floating upwards. "Imagine yourself flying towards the top of that cliff. Imagine that you've been doing it for years. Picture it in your head, and your wings will adapt to that picture. It's silly I know, but it's the easiest way."

Ben did a backflip in the air. "Hey, I think I've got it!" He started falling rapidly. "Concentrate!" Marcus yelled. Ben stopped falling, and Marcus flew up to where he was. "Now, let's go." He started flying quickly, up towards the top of the cliff. Ben followed with a new sense of confidence. He was no longer flying sideways. He looked back down at the ground and smiled. They reached the top of the cliff, landed safely on the edge, and let their wings shrink into their backs. Ben looked up ahead of him and saw a white glowing staircase ascending into the clouds. "You mean there actually *is* a Stairway to Heaven?" he asked.

"Of course," Marcus replied. "Where do you think Robert Plant got the idea? Lucifer pretty much *wrote* the song. They're old friends."

"Why can't you just teleport us there? Like you did from my house to here? I'm an angel now, right?"

"Because I can't 'teleport' between Heaven and Earth. Not until I find my sword."

They started walking up the staircase towards the clouds. When they reached the top, Ben looked up at the Pearly Gates in front of him. He saw an old bearded angel sitting to the side, reading a book. The angel looked up and saw Ben and Marcus approach. "Marcus!" he said, "You're not supposed to be here!"

"Relax old man, I'll be right out."

"And what's this? You can't bring a human in."

"Ben, wings!" Ben's' wings rose up out of his back.

The angel looked Ben up and down. "Nonetheless, I can't let you pass."

Marcus gave him a fiery look. "Try to stop me, Peter." Peter went to speak, but stopped. He knew that if he were to take on Marcus, he would surely lose. Although he used to be a great warrior once upon a time, he knew that he wouldn't stand a chance against Marcus, even in his younger days. "Go on, but come straight out." Marcus threw the gates open. They walked in.

Ben stood in awe as they stepped through the gates. He saw an immaculate city of white, with buildings made of something like pearl on both sides of a blue street. He knelt down and felt the ground with his fingers. "It's just like carpet," he said. He looked at all the faces around him. Everyone had a look of happiness on their faces, and Ben felt like a small child who had just met Santa Claus. He smiled. "It's beautiful! I mean, I imagined it would be something like this, but the real thing has still managed to top my imagination." Marcus started walking quickly down the street with determination. He had to be in and out as quickly as possible. "Where are we going?" Ben asked.

"I need to speak with somebody," Marcus replied.

Ben didn't say another word. He had an idea who Marcus needed to speak with. They came to the end of the blue carpet-like street, and found themselves standing at the bottom of a staircase that was obviously made from the same material as the buildings surrounding them. A large muscular angel who was standing close by, began moving quickly towards them. "Marcus!" he called, "What are you doing here?"

"I came to speak with him."

"Well, obviously. It's good to see you."

"You too, Michael."

Ben looked up at Michael. His arms were like tree trunks, he had no hair, and he had a welcoming face. His voice was very low and calming. "You're the Archangel Michael!" he said.

"Yes, I am," Michael replied. "You must be Ben. Very pleased to finally meet you."

"What do you mean, finally?"

"Well, you're not exactly a secret. Everybody here knows about you. You were chosen to become an angel, and to assist Marcus. That's not very common. And, he has trained you. Which, in my opinion, there is no greater teacher."

Marcus stepped in. "That's enough, Michael. You're treating me like royalty here. Have we forgotten that *you* trained *me*?"

"Why else would there be no greater teacher?"

Marcus turned to Ben. "Michael fought side by side with my father and my uncle."

"Well then, the pleasure is all mine," Ben said.

Michael gestured up the staircase. "He's waiting for you," he said.

Marcus set one foot on the bottom step, and then half turned around to Ben. "Wait here, okay?" Ben nodded. Marcus turned and walked up the stairs. At the very top, he kneeled before God. God stood up from his seat and walked over to Marcus. He placed his hand on Marcus' shoulder. "Welcome home, my Son," he said.

* * *

Beelzebub was sitting on his throne, atop a large staircase inside his cave in Purgatory. There were smaller devils around the cave, standing against the wall. The room was circular, with the staircase at one end, and the entrance from Purgatory at the other. There were also two other doorways either side of the staircase. Beelzebub looked down at a shrouded figure standing at the bottom of the stairs as he awaited the news. "It's begun," the figure said, "He's got the human, and he's persuaded Lucifer to join him. Lucifer's two underlings have also agreed to go."

The devil let out a faint growl. "Don't worry, I'll send someone," he said.

"Who, exactly?" the figure hesitantly asked.

"I'll send Baal, if I need to."

The figure stepped back. "I'm not comfortable with that. He never took kindly to me," the figure replied.

The devil gave a half lopsided grin. "So, keep your distance." The figure left the cave and headed out to Purgatory.

"Orias! Eligos!" the devil shouted. A large hulking figure emerged from the right of the staircase. He looked almost human, but was enormous. His muscular body was covered in archaic tattoos and he had large black leathery wings, two horns protruding out of his forehead, and very long turquoise hair. In his left hand was a large stone; one he used to bludgeon his enemies, and also to sharpen the dagger in his right hand. The blade on the dagger was about fourteen inches long, and stuck out of his closed fist behind him, below the knuckles. He was very skilled with his dagger. Orias was an Incubus. Most stories of Incubi tell of their seduction, to prey on women, as a way of sucking their life-force, which is true, yet only one of their many abilities. Their counterpart, the Succubi, prey on men.

As Orias emerged from the doorway to the right, Eligos, not just any Succubus, *the* Succubus, emerged from the doorway to the left. She wasn't quite as big as Orias, but definitely looked as scary. Many would consider her the Queen of the Succubi, as she had been around for thousands of years, and was adept at what she did. She once even suckered the mighty Arus. She too, had tattoos all over her muscular body, horns protruding from her forehead, and large black leathery wings. They both had grey skin and tattered clothing. Orias wore only pants and big black boots, while Eligos had a black leathery looking outfit, which left little to the imagination. They were an elite force, that had never come up against anything that opposed them. Only Marcus had ever escaped their clutches, and they had vowed for the day they would get to hunt him again. They stepped forward and stood before the steps leading up to Beelzebub. He looked down at them both, shifting his gaze from one to the other. Orias held his dagger in front of his face and ran the stone along the blade with a quick *shunk* sound. It was something he did very often, as he never knew when he was going to need his dagger, and he always liked it to remain sharp - just in case.

"I'm sending you both after Marcus. You two finally get to hunt your ultimate prize. Go!" They both leaped into the air and took off in flight out of the cave and into Purgatory, as Baal stepped forward. "Want me to go? Just in case?" he asked. Baal was a devil, similar to Beelzebub, but nowhere near as powerful. He was slightly smaller in size, and had more of a brown, almost black colour to his scaly skin, whereas Beelzebub was more a reddish brown. He was the right-hand man, second in charge after the devil himself. Baal was a devil, but Beelzebub was *the* devil. "Are you necessary?" the devil asked.

Baal gave a smug devilish grin. "Well, I'm stronger than those two."

"Against Marcus, she's stronger."

Baal tilted his head in confusion. "I beg to differ," he reasoned. "How so?"

"Because no offspring of Arus is allowed to harm her."

Baal still pondered the argument in confusion, as the devil continued. "The child, the Nephilim. When Arus and the human woman had the child, it was Eligos who helped him, but not without a price."

"I still don't understand the price. Marcus isn't allowed to kill her. So, what if he does?"

The devil gave an evil smile. "He'll become the Archfiend."

* * *

Marcus looked up at God, who looked at him like a father looks at his newborn child. With glistening short white hair, and blue eyes looking down, Marcus felt it was like a ray of sunshine beaming down upon him. Gods' platinum wings rose up out of his back. "Come, walk with me. There is much we need to discuss."

Marcus stood up and followed God down a set of steps to the right of the throne. They stepped off the bottom step into a white courtyard, with ivy growing up the pillars around it, and a medium size fountain in the middle. They sat side by side on a bench. "I don't know if I can do this," Marcus said.

"Don't know if you can? Or don't know if you should?"

"Okay, I know I can. But, what will become of this? Where will this take me? Will this sword really help us? I know when you kicked me out, you wrote the Revelation as a loophole, but why me? Am I really that important?"

"You doubt yourself too much. When you gain confidence, you will find the answers will come to you. I can't give them all to you. All I can do is guide you along the way. I show you the door, you have to walk through it."

"What is the benefit of the sword? Why do we need it that badly?"

"When the time comes, you will know why it is needed. The answers are already in your head. You just need to find the keys to unlock them. Marcus, you created the sword. No greater sword has ever been created, and its power comes from he who created it. The most powerful sword must belong to the most powerful angel."

"So, you're saying I'm the most powerful angel?"

"I'm not saying that. You know that when the chosen Commander of Battle creates a sword, the sword becomes however powerful the angel is, or will become. The reason we need the sword right now is because without it, there is no Commander of Battle. And to be honest with you, I think our opposition has figured that out."

"So, I can either retire my position, and let somebody else create a sword and become the Commander of Battle, or I can go and find my sword, and take up the position that was given to me."

"What does the Revelation say you should do?"

Marcus took a deep breath. "The Revelation says I should find my sword," he said.

"And what do you think you should do?"
"I think I should find my sword." Marcus said as he looked up at God.

"Well then, go get it Son."

Marcus nodded. They both stood up, and God put his hand on Marcus' shoulder. "I know you can do this; regardless of whether you think you can or not. Know that."

"Thank you," Marcus said as he turned to walk back up the steps.

"And, don't storm in here again. Don't forget, you must find that sword before you come back."

"Yeah, yeah," he said over his shoulder. He walked past the throne and down the steps towards Michael and Ben. "Let's go," he said.

"Where to, now?" Ben asked.

"To get my sword." He turned to Michael. "Always good to see you, Michael."

"Good luck, my friends," Michael said as he turned to walk away. God came back up from the courtyard and sat on his throne. His platinum wings swayed above him. "Is that who I think it is?" Ben asked.

"I think you already know the answer to that question," Marcus replied as he nodded to God, and turned to walk back towards the gates. Dumbfounded, Ben waved to God, who nodded in return. Ben turned to follow Marcus. He ran to catch up with him. Marcus walked quickly towards the gate. He had determination in his blue eyes. "Why are you walking so fast?" Ben asked.

"I'm not supposed to be here, remember?" Marcus sped up. They got closer to the gate. Heads turned as they walked past. "Everybody is looking at us," Ben said awkwardly.

"Don't worry about it," Marcus said. They walked out of the gates and down the staircase to the top of the cliff. They stopped for a moment and looked out over the hills of Wyoming. Ben looked at Marcus. "I'm confused. Arus is supposed to be old, and from what I've gathered, one of the top angels. I mean, I've heard of Michael, Gabriel, Lucifer, Raphael. I've never heard of Arus."

"Arus is Raphael."

"So why is he called Arus?" Ben asked.

Marcus shrugged. "Why am I called Marcus?" he asked. Ben raised an eyebrow as Marcus opened his wings, and Ben took the hint and opened his own. They leapt off the top of the cliff and slowly descended down to the earth. They saw Azazel, Asmodeus, and Lucifer waiting for them at the bottom of Devils Tower.

"So, how was it? Still the same?" Lucifer asked.

"Still the same, Michael says hello," Marcus replied.

"No, he doesn't."

"Oh yeah, I guess not. So, let's go."

"Okay," Lucifer said, "We can walk from here."

Marcus stopped. "To the garden? From here?" he asked.

"No," Lucifer replied, "to the airport. We need to get to the museum."

"Museum?" Marcus looked irritable.

"Of course! We need the staff."

"What staff?" Ben asked.

"The Staff of Moses! What, were you born yesterday?"

"Lucifer," Marcus put his hands on Lucifer's' shoulders, "you need to be really clear with me here. Why do we need the Staff of Moses?"

Lucifer looked blankly at Marcus. "Is this some sort of test?"

Marcus shook Lucifer. "Just answer the question!"
"Okay, geez!" Lucifer fixed his clothes up. "We need the staff to find Eden."

"To find it? I thought you knew where it was!" Marcus said angrily.

"I never said that," he said smugly. "I know how to get there, but I never said I knew where it was. No one knows where it is. Let's walk and talk." They started walking.

"So, how do we get there?" Marcus asked. His eyes were filling with more anger every second; his eyebrows pointing straight down towards his nose.

"Well," Lucifer began, "when you don't want anybody to find a certain thing or place, what do you do?"

"You hide it," Ben said from the back.

"Precisely!" Lucifer continued. "You hide it from everyone and everything, so that even those who have been there couldn't find it."

Lucifer stared at Marcus. "And suppose you knew that someday, you would need somebody to go find it for you. What would you do?"

"I'd show them how to get there," Marcus replied.

"Exactly." Lucifer basked in his ego.
"But, I wasn't shown, was I?"

"Of course you weren't, you idiot. I was."

"You?" Marcus asked in disbelief. "But how? Why?"

"He has his reasons. Surely you can understand that it's easier to show somebody that's already been there, right?"

"I guess so," Marcus said.

"What led you to believe I knew where it was?" Lucifer asked.

Marcus looked at Lucifer with a half-smile. Lucifer caught on. "Mr. Fancy Pants? I told you not to listen to a word he says!" They continued walking in the dark.

"Where's this museum then?" Marcus asked.

"In Birmingham. We'll have to catch a plane to London in the morning," Lucifer said.

"A plane?" Ben asked, "Why don't we just use our wings and fly? It'll take us hours by plane!"

"Fly?" Lucifer replied, "And risk being seen?"

"We can fly at night, can't we?"
"Our wings are luminous, boy. We'd be even more visible at night." Lucifer looked over at Marcus. "Take him back to angel school, eh?"

"So, what should we do then?" Ben asked.

"Well, since we've got some time to kill, I say we check out the local waterhole," Marcus replied.

"There you go, off to your drinking again. I was thinking of something a little more fun. Who wants to make some money?" Lucifer asked. They walked down a staircase into an underground room. It was filled with men surrounding a large circle in the middle of the room, yelling at the two men in the middle fighting for their lives. The circle in the middle was lower than the rest of the floor. The men surrounding it were standing on a down slope facing the middle. Lucifer breathed in. "Ahh, now, this will be fun!" he shouted over the noise.

"You wouldn't last five seconds in there," Marcus said.

"I never said I was going in there," Lucifer replied.

"Well, I ain't fighting humans for fun, or for money."

"You don't have to," Lucifer said slyly. "Azazel! Come make us some money."

Azazel walked with a large stride and an angry face. Lucifer walked up to the back of the crowd with Azazel by his side. The fight in front of them persisted. Blood spattered all over the floor; punch after punch, kick after kick. Sweat poured off their bodies and onto the ground, making it almost reflective. "These places are brutal," Marcus said to Ben. "Anything goes. These poor humans. Azazel will liquefy them." The fight finished with a mighty punch, and a loud roar from the crowd. The referee checked the man's pulse and stood up waving his arms, pronouncing the man's death. The crowd cheered. The referee spoke: "Once again, our champion undefeated!" He spoke with a broad English accent that matched his largely built size. "Do we have another challenger to take on the title?"

Lucifer went to open his mouth but was beaten to the punch. "Challenge!" Marcus shouted from the back. Everybody turned around slowly to see where the voice came from, even Lucifer. Marcus was leaning against the back wall near the steps. There was silence in the room. All eyes were on Marcus. "Challenge," he said again. The entire crowd laughed at his size and turned around waiting for a real challenger. Lucifer saw his opportunity. "A thousand bucks on the little guy!" he shouted. The men all turned around to see Lucifer with a wad of cash in his hands, and just as swiftly turned around again to eagerly place large bets on their champion. They separated and formed an aisle for Marcus to walk down. Marcus walked past Ben and Asmodeus, and then past Azazel and Lucifer.

"What are you doing?" Lucifer asked. "I thought you wouldn't fight humans."

"I won't," Marcus replied as he kept walking. He made his way past the angry faces staring at him, to the hollowed-out circle in the middle. His opponent was facing away from him with a towel on his head. He removed the towel and turned around slowly. He was about 6'5, and built like Lucifer's' butler. He saw Marcus and recognised him instantly. He stepped back in fear. He squinted and stepped forward again to double check if it was Marcus. "What are you doing here?" he asked Marcus.

"I should ask you the same question. I told you I would kill you if I caught you doing this again."

The man turned to the referee. "I'm not fighting him. He's crazy! He'll kill me!" he said.

"Anything goes, remember?" Marcus said.

He lunged at the man with a fast and strong right fist. It landed hard on the man's left cheek. He went down quickly. The crowd gasped and looked on in silence. The man spat out some blood as he struggled up on to his knees, and then planted one foot on the ground. He tried to outwit Marcus by swinging a big uppercut, but Marcus blocked and stepped to the man's side. He swung a hard punch to the man's temple.

He went down again. Marcus stood back to let the man rejuvenate. A sword instantly appeared in the man's hand, and the crowd stared in awe. The man ran at Marcus with the sword, charging as fast as he could. The sword was pointing straight out and heading for Marcus like a lance. Lucifer looked on with a smile on his face, and a glint in his eye. He knew that Marcus had already won this fight, as soon as the man pulled the sword. Lucifer recognised him now, and realised why Marcus decided to fight him.

The man kept charging at Marcus. The sword was straight out in front of him, and his arms were at their full extent. All eyes were on the blade to see what would happen next. Marcus stepped to the side and kicked the man in the chest. He used all his body force and channeled it into the sole of his foot, which was now flat against the man's chest. At the same time, Marcus grabbed the flat of the blade with both palms to avoid being cut. The man's face quickly turned a deep blue. All the air had been knocked out of him. Marcus put one hand near the tip of the blade, and the other near the middle and started pushing. The blade started bending in half, whilst the man still had hold of the handle. Marcus kicked the man again, who let go of the handle of the sword and went tumbling backwards. He fell on his back in agony. The crowd cheered. Marcus still had hold of the sword by the blade. It was completely curved into a perfect "U" shape. He stared at it. "What a piece of shit!" Marcus shrieked as he tossed it up lightly into the air. It reached the same height his shoulder, and then dropped to the ground. He walked over to the man lying on his back. He knelt down and whispered into his ear.

"I warned you, and you completely disregarded that. To me, that's an insult. No demon can engage in mortal combat with humans. Punishment is complete and utter death. Any last words?"

The man opened his mouth and tried to speak.

"I'm s... so.. sorr..."

Marcus put his hand on the man's mouth. He turned his head all the way to the side, facing away from him. He gripped the back of the man's head with his other hand, and violently snapped it back towards him. A clean break. "I didn't think so." Marcus said. He stood up and walked through the group of men and past his companions. He found his way to the stairs and walked up. Ben followed Marcus. Lucifer watched them leave, and then turned around to face the crowd. "Pay up," he said. The man handling the money came up to Lucifer and hesitantly put a large wad of cash in his hand. "Can I ask you a question?" the cash handler asked.

Lucifer looked him up and down. "Well you didn't give me much choice there, did you? What you should have asked is 'Can I ask you *two* questions?' But you didn't. What if I'd said no? Right mistake that was, wasn't it?"

"OK, I'm sorry. Two questions. The second one is where did you dig him up?"

"He's my brother. And I think you're the one that needs to do some digging." He motioned to the body lying on the floor. "Good day gentlemen, and thank you for your time."
Lucifer turned and walked up the stairs. Azazel and Asmodeus followed. Marcus was sitting down on the ground near the entrance as Lucifer walked out. "Well, that was fun," he said with a smile.

"Fun?" Ben asked. "How was that fun? Marcus just killed a man in cold blood!"

"No, I didn't," Marcus defended.

"What kind of angels are you? You know they have no chance against you," Ben pleaded.

"Ben," Marcus said, "he wasn't human. He was a demon, and I had a score to settle."

"Really?" Ben asked. "He was a demon?"

Marcus nodded. Ben looked at Lucifer who also nodded. He then looked at Azazel and Asmodeus. "You two don't talk much, do you?" he asked.

"Not really," Asmodeus said, "only when we really need to. Otherwise it's just a waste of breath." He had a very light, almost upper class British sort of voice. Ben was surprised.

"Come on," Marcus said. "Let's get some rest."

CHAPTER III

They walked out of the town and into the wilderness, and found a secluded spot where there was nobody for miles. They sat down and got comfortable. Lucifer, Ben, Azazel, and Asmodeus were sitting in a clearing, whilst Marcus was sitting up against a tree. He was staring into oblivion, thinking about the journey that lay ahead of him. The other four talked about whatever crossed their minds. "To be brutally honest," Lucifer said, "He was a git. Never did anything but battle humans for money. Lived on earth like a king. Thankfully, Marcus sent him back to Purgatory."

"Purgatory?" Ben asked. "What do you mean?"

"When an angel is killed by anyone who opposes him, he goes to purgatory. Same for demons." Azazel said with his cockney accent.

"Purgatory is a place of death and decay. You think Hell is bad? That place makes Hell look like ice cream," Lucifer added.

"So, how did you get to see it?" Ben asked.

"Well," Lucifer started, "an angel found his way in there and then transported back to Heaven and showed others. Marcus showed me."

"Transport?" Ben asked.

"It's what we call it. We can instantly transport ourselves to any location, providing we've been there before or know what it looks like. And in some cases, we can transport somewhere just by thinking of something that's at that location. It's a strange concept, but easy nonetheless," Lucifer explained.

"Okay then," Ben said, "so who was the angel that went in?"

"I don't know. I haven't been to Heaven since Eden."

"I heard he didn't transport out. I heard he was killed, sent to Purgatory, then he got out through the caves," Azazel said.

"Nonsense!" Lucifer scoffed. "No one has been through those caves and lived to talk about it."

"Can I see it?" Ben asked Lucifer.

"No," Marcus said from his spot in front of the tree. "It's too dangerous."

"Dangerous? How?" Ben asked.

"Ben, if you die in Purgatory, you die for good. No Heaven, no Hell, just the cease of existence. Nothingness." Marcus explained.

"Oh," Ben replied. "Perhaps we can leave that for another day." He blew out a deep breath. "So, why are we walking everywhere? And sleeping in the wilderness? Why don't we just transport?"

"Because we have nowhere to stay, and angels can't touch the Staff of Moses. You're the closest thing to a human that we've got, and you haven't used any of your gifts as of yet. If you transport, then you won't be able to touch it," Lucifer said.

"He's right Ben. You haven't learnt how to transport yet. Best you learn after we find my sword. That way if we need a human along the way, we can use you."

"But I'm an angel now. And I have identification, and Lucifer has money," Ben said.

"I suppose we could live it up in hotels, and technically you're still a human; you just have wings. You haven't officially become an angel yet. That's probably why Eran said we need you. And why I said it I suppose," Marcus said.

"But, you didn't know we needed the Staff of Moses," Ben said.

"Among other things," Lucifer mumbled to himself.
"What was that?" Marcus asked as he stood up.

"What?" Lucifer replied.

"Don't play games with me. What else do we need?"

"Okay, this is where I need *your* help. Do you still know where the Ark of the Covenant is?"

"Of course I do. I carried it to Ethiopia. Why?"

"Because we need to find that too."

"What is this?" Marcus asked, "A treasure hunt?"

"There's certain things we need to get to Eden," Lucifer replied.

Marcus kicked a stone across the ground. "I didn't expect to be digging up artifacts. I just want to get my sword." There was silence among them.

"You carried the Ark of the Covenant to Ethiopia?" Ben asked.

"Yes, God asked me to take it out of Jerusalem. He said it would be guarded well there, and no one but the guardian has ever laid eyes on it. Not even the High Priests," Marcus replied.

"Who is the guardian?" Ben asked.

"He is an angel in human form. When the carrying body gets too old, he appoints another to take over for when it dies. Kind of like a buffet. He lives in the chapel and never leaves. He doesn't let anybody else even take a peak."

"So, how are we going to get to it?" Lucifer asked.

"Easy. They don't let anybody look at it because they were told not to... by angels. We fly in with our wings wide open, tell them what we need, leave them a few words of wisdom, and go."

"How do you know all of this?" Lucifer asked.

"Because I'm the angel who told them what to do," Marcus said.

They all looked at each other. There was a deafening silence in the air, broken only by the sounds of the wilderness. Marcus decided to break it. "So, is that all? What else do we need?"

Lucifer looked sideways at Marcus. "I thought you'd be able to answer that," he said. Marcus looked at Ben. He shifted his eyes to the pendant around Ben's neck. It looked like a steel shark's tooth hanging below his sternal notch on a steel chain. It was carefully crafted, almost as if finely sanded, yet the top looked like it was chipped off of something. Marcus had seen it around Ben's neck before, but he had seen it somewhere before he saw Ben with it; long before Ben was even born. Marcus used to wear it around his own neck. He gave it to his father when he came down to earth to find his sword. He knew his father would keep it safe. Marcus sat in thought as he stared at it. He began to realise that it was actually the Amulet of the Shadows, and he never really took notice. After learning about Ben's lineage, it finally made sense. "We need this," Marcus said as he flicked the pendant.

"What for?" Lucifer asked. "What is that?"

Marcus opened his eyes wider. He stared at the pendant, unable to move his eyes. "It's the Amulet of the Shadows," he said.

"You're kidding!" Lucifer gasped. "You can't be serious! Are you?"

"Of course, I'm serious. I should know my own handy work when I see it."

Ben stepped back. "Your own handy work? My dad gave me this!" he said.

"And I gave it to my father, who obviously gave it to Amalie," Marcus replied.

"What?" Ben shrieked. "I'm starting to get really pissed off at all these coincidences. First, one of my ancestors is your father, meaning I'm half angel or whatever, and now this entire time, you suddenly realise I'm wearing something you gave to Arus years ago? What is its significance?"

"It's nothing, Ben. I'm pretty sure we're going to need light at some point, which the amulet can provide. From what I can understand, we need the Staff of Moses, and the Ark of the Covenant to part water. But the only reason we would need to part water is if the Garden is underwater."

Marcus glanced at Lucifer. "It's under the Persian Gulf, isn't it?" he asked.

"What makes you think that? I may just want some artefacts for my collection," Lucifer smirked.

Marcus grabbed Lucifer by the collar, picked him up, and slammed him into a tree. "Don't toy with me!" Marcus said through his teeth.

Lucifer rolled his eyes and returned Marcus' stare. "Yes, it's under the Persian Gulf," he sighed.'

Marcus lifted one eyebrow. "You know what that lies between, don't you? We'd be walking into a mortal war-zone, and there are a fair few demons that have made a good home there. They just might recognise us," he said.

Lucifer grabbed Marcus' hand and pulled it away from his collar with great effort.

"That's why we travel by sea," he replied. "We just need enough money to buy a boat."

"Why do we need to buy one?" Azazel shouted. "It's not like we can be arrested."

"You seem to forget who you're tagging along with," Marcus replied, "and I'm not a thief."

"Who gives a flying toss?" Azazel stood up and walked towards Marcus.

"Azazel, no." Lucifer said. "Don't even try."

Azazel stopped. He looked at Marcus, then at Lucifer, then stared back at Marcus. Marcus returned his stare. "He's not going to protect you forever, pretty boy!" Azazel said to Marcus as he turned around and sat down again. Marcus looked at Lucifer. He stepped in close towards him and whispered in his ear. "Why is he under the impression that I need your protection?" he asked.

"Because he doubts your ability," Lucifer replied.

"Does he now? Even *you* haven't seen me lately."

Lucifer looked at Marcus in deep thought. His little brother was growing up. He had obviously spent a lot of time in America, as he had adapted the accent, and pulled it off well. He had changed clothing styles many times, and Lucifer had seen them all. The 1980's were the worst. Some of the outfits he would visit in were just appalling. But Lucifer stood back and had to admire the angel his brother was becoming. His curly brown hair did cartwheels in the wind, his brown jacket looked very modern. The black hood hanging out of the back of his collar was flapping back and forth between his head and shoulders in the wind. His blue eyes that matched the colour of his jeans stared through Lucifer as if he wasn't even there. He had seen far too much to gain a stare like that. Lucifer lightly punched him on the shoulder. "I'm sure we'll all get to see it soon," Lucifer said with a smile. "We'll buy a boat, and travel by sea. That's how it has to be done."

Marcus nodded as Lucifer turned towards Azazel and Asmodeus, and resumed his seat amongst them. Marcus walked back to his tree and put his back up against it. He slid down into a sitting position, rested the back of his head against the tree, and closed his eyes. He opened them as soon as he sensed Ben sitting in front of him. Ben was staring at him with a thousand questions in his eyes. "What?" Marcus asked.

"This doesn't make any sense. I don't get any of this," Ben replied.

"At this point, the less you know, the better. I don't even know enough about it. All I know is that my sword is in a place that can't be found, and by gathering old artefacts that did something once, I'll find it."

"You see? It doesn't add up. I think there's something we're not being told. Do you think Lucifer is telling you the truth?"
"I know he is. He doesn't lie to me, he's my brother. He knows he can trust me, and that I can beat the hell out of him."

"So, what then?"

Marcus looked at the ground. He now had a thousand questions running through his head. "I'll be back," he said. He jumped up and opened his wings. "Marcus, don't leave me alone with them!" Ben loudly whispered.

"Lucifer will take care of you. And if he doesn't, I'll take care of him. He knows that. Wait here."

With that, Marcus took off. The blue glow from his wings lingered in the air, then faded back to darkness. Ben sat in between Lucifer and Asmodeus. "Don't leave me alone with them!" Asmodeus mimicked. Both Asmodeus and Azazel laughed. Ben stood up and picked up a large fallen branch off the ground. He stood directly in between the fire and the two of them and swung at them from the right like it was a golf club. It slammed into the side of Asmodeus' face and kept moving towards Azazel. Azazel saw it coming, but Ben's swing was too fast. It struck him on the chin as he fell over from his sitting position. Ben stood upright and threw the branch one handed to his side. "Shut the hell up!" he shouted. He sat back down next to Lucifer with his eyebrows pointing directly at the bridge in his nose, as he stared at the open fire in front of him. Lucifer stared in awe. He didn't believe what had just happened. Asmodeus and Azazel sat upright and rubbed their faces and looked over at Ben in unison. Their eyes filled with anger. "Oh you're fantastic!" Lucifer shouted. "You can tell who taught you!"

Ben laughed. "He kind of rubs off on you doesn't he?" he replied. He looked over at Asmodeus and Azazel still rubbing their faces. "You two play nice okay? We're supposed to be on the same team here," Ben said sternly.

They both stopped rubbing their faces. "We're not scared of you, ya little toss pot!" Azazel shouted. Ben smiled with a new sense of confidence. *Think like Marcus*, he thought. "Good, I'd prefer it that way. Gives you the element of surprise!" he said, with his eyes slowly bouncing between the two.

* * *

"Wake up!" Marcus shouted at the four of them. He had returned to find them all asleep around the burning embers remaining from the fire. They all half sat up and became familiar with their surroundings. They looked up at Marcus in turn, standing in the gap closing the circle of their little huddle. His wings lit up the wilderness around them a bright eerie blue. "Where in the *hell* have you been?" Ben asked.

"Not hell, Earth. Have a nice sleep?"

Azazel and Asmodeus looked at Ben and then back up at Marcus. "He hit us!" Azazel muttered pointing at Ben.

"You gonna cry? He's a fucking human!"

Ben looked up at Marcus. "You know, for an angel, you swear a bit too much. And I thought I was an angel now," he said.

"No, you're a human angel hybrid with wings. First born in your bloodline. Apparently because you are destined to help the side of good, you have been granted status. But because you didn't die, and haven't been properly taken into the kingdom of Heaven, you aren't an angel. And that's exactly how we need you," Marcus replied.

Ben wiped his forehead and shook his head. "Yeah, that makes sense," he said sarcastically.

"It's simple," Marcus said. "You will become an angel. Just not yet. Right now we need a human, and you're the closest thing we've got. Now let's go."

Lucifer sat up. "Go?" he asked. "Where?"

"First of all, we don't need the Staff of Moses. We're in the wrong place," Marcus replied.

Lucifer looked at Marcus in astonishment. "No. No, that can't be right. I was told. The Staff of Moses and the Ark of the Covenant!" he shouted.

"Ahh, but do you think we would be told the whole story?" Marcus asked.

"You saying he told me wrong?"

"I'm saying he gave you a riddle."

"That's ridiculous. Who told you this?" Lucifer had his eyes wide open, waiting for an answer. He almost wasn't going to get one until Marcus decided to speak. "Who do I always ask about these things?"

Lucifer closed his eyes and sat still for a long moment. He opened them again. "How is he?" he asked.

"He's the same as last time. Still hibernating in some cave."

Ben tilted his head to the side like a dog does when it hears a strange noise. "You went to see Arus?" Ben asked.

"How does he do that?" Lucifer asked. "He always figures everything out!"

"It's why he's here," Marcus replied. *"Now* can we go?"

Asmodeus stomped on the remains of the fire and they all got ready to head off. "So where are we headed?" Ben asked.

Marcus smiled. "Your house."

"I thought I wasn't supposed to be transported," Ben said, standing out the front of his own house.

"That's what else I found out. You can. You just can't do it yourself," Marcus replied.

"Right."

It was still pitch black. They all walked into Ben's house. He turned on the inside light. It was a nice place, with cream painted walls. The lounge room was on the right, and the kitchen bench was next to the front door on the left. Very open plan. Ben was happy to be home, but he didn't really feel like he had a home any more. His life had completely changed in the past twenty four hours. So many things had taken over so quickly, that he barely even recognised the place. He set his keys down on the kitchen bench just to the left of the doorway. "Come on Marcus, what are we doing here?" Lucifer asked.

Marcus put his hand up with his finger pointing straight up, as if to ask for silence. "Ben, go get your favourite weapon," he said.

Ben looked towards the hallway, which was on the other side of the kitchen. "Why do I need that?" he asked. Marcus used a look Ben had seen many times before. It was his *just do it* look, and it always worked. Ben walked through the kitchen and into the hallway. He took the second door on the left into a room full of all kinds of weapons. The walls were covered in an assortment of swords, knives, guns and other various items. But, there was only one bow staff - his favourite weapon. His pride and joy. Marcus was into swords. Ben and Marcus both knew that with this bow staff, Ben could even beat Marcus. He slowly and carefully took it off the wall. He held the hemp grip with his left hand and ran his right hand along it. It was like being reacquainted with an old friend. It had a leather strap at one end of the grip for it to be slung over his shoulder. He looked out the door and quickly flipped it into his right hand. He walked back out through the kitchen and into the lounge room. Lucifer looked at the bow staff. "That's what we came here for?" he chuckled. "This piece of wood?"

Within two seconds, Ben had him up against the wall with the bow staff under his chin. Lucifer gasped and gagged with a stunned look in his eyes. Ben released his grip and helped Lucifer down. "And what a fine piece of wood it is!" he remarked, while holding his throat.

Lucifer looked at Marcus. "He's pretty fast," he stated.

"Okay," Marcus said, "we have to leave now."

Everyone stared at Marcus. "Why? What's the big hurry?" Lucifer asked. "Your sword will still be there when we get there."

"No," Marcus said, "we're being watched."

They all looked around themselves, trying to figure out what Marcus meant. Lucifer noticed that Marcus hadn't shifted his gaze from the large glass window at the back of the lounge room. "By who?" he asked.

Marcus stared out the window. "No, not by who," Marcus said, "by *what*." They all turned to look out the glass window just in time to see a large red figure burst through it. It fell to a crouch and slowly stood up. It was enormous, with big black menacing eyes, large sharp teeth, almost piranha-like. It moved closer to them and snarled. It had large claws on the end of long wrinkled fingers. "What the hell is that thing, and what is it doing in my house?" Ben yelled.

"What does it look like?" Marcus screamed back, as he drew his sword and lunged himself in front of everybody else. Marcus was quick. But even this demon supposedly threw him off guard. In a split second, the demon was next to him, and he was thrown across the room hitting the far side wall of the lounge room. The demon stared at Ben. Asmodeus looked around for a quick escape as Azazel readied himself to take on the giant beast. He stepped forward. The demon hit him with a forearm to the head. He went tumbling backwards towards the door. Ben ran over to Marcus to help him up. Marcus looked up at the demon following all of Ben's moves. "Bless the staff!" he shouted.

Ben looked sideways at Marcus. He stood up and looked at his bow staff in his hand. "Oh, let me!" Marcus grumbled. He grabbed the staff with his right hand, letting Ben still keep hold of it, and put his left hand on Ben's head. "In the name of God, I deem this the Staff of Ben. Let him use it with all the power of the angels." The staff gave off a faint yellow glow. Marcus let go of it. "Go! Take him out!" he shouted.

Ben looked up at the demon. It moved towards him slowly and breathed heavily. It gave off a wheezing sound as it breathed, almost like it was breathing for the first time. It lunged itself at Ben. With a quick flick, he hit the demon in the head with his bow staff. The demon fell down and quickly got back up. It swiped at Ben. He blocked the swing with one end of the staff and quickly brought the other end up and smashed it into the demon's face. The demon stumbled backwards, and Ben kept swinging. He spun a full circle, swiped the staff at the demon's legs and it fell over. In the same swift move, he hit it on the side of the head with the other end. The demon fell down, dazed.

"Kill it!" Lucifer shouted. "While you have a chance!"

Ben stood at the demons head and held his staff, almost like an oversized golf club. He raised it above his head and quickly swung the staff. It snapped the demons head straight off. Both the head and body burst into a pasty, cement-like liquid and settled into a grey puddle on the floor. Ben took a deep breath of accomplishment and awe both at the same time . He walked to the kitchen and grabbed a cloth. He began cleaning his staff. Lucifer watched his every move. "Oh! Idiot!" he said.

"What?" Ben asked confidently.

"Not you," he replied, "me." He turned to Marcus. "An enchanted staff to part the waters; not the Staff of Moses. But it has to be bound to a human. That's what he told you, right?" Lucifer asked.

"He didn't tell me anything. You should know that better than anyone," Marcus replied.

"Good point. Just like old times."

"Yeah, just like new times too."

Ben looked at Marcus. "I can't believe you couldn't take him out!" he said.

Marcus looked at Ben. "As if I couldn't." he said. "I was just giving you experience in killing one of these things. Now you know you can."

Marcus stared down at the cement-like puddle. Lucifer walked over to it and put the toe of his leather boot in it. It moved under his boot like mud. He looked at Marcus. "Do you think he'll send more?" he asked Marcus.

"Without a doubt. What I don't get is how they knew we'd come here," Marcus replied.

"They could have followed us," Ben said.

"No," Lucifer cut him off. "You can't follow through instant transporting."

"Well, there are only five of us who knew we were coming here," Ben barked back.

"Six," Marcus said. "I told Arus."

"He doesn't count," Lucifer said. "He doesn't talk to anyone."

"And Ben and I don't count, because we wouldn't send a demon after ourselves," Marcus said.

Lucifer looked at Marcus. "What, you think I had something to do with this?" he asked.

"No, not you," Marcus said as he shifted his focus to Azazel and Asmodeus.

"Oi!" Azazel shouted. "You look at me like that, I'll break ya face!"

Marcus rolled his eyes. "You couldn't break a sweat!" Marcus snapped.

The already growing tension between them grew a little more. Azazel stayed quiet and just glared at Marcus. He couldn't think of anything to say back. Lucifer knew that Marcus was crazy when it came to fighting. He had never seen him beaten, but once. And, even that was hardly fair. He was small and thin, but he had such strength; such fierce nature. Such a flame burned inside him. He knew that Marcus would not even flinch at the slightest sign of an actual challenge. But Azazel would be a worthy opponent. He was short, but wide. To see a fight between Marcus and Azazel would be a sight to see. But, Lucifer didn't get to see that.

"Well, I can tell it's not you," Marcus said smugly. He looked over at Asmodeus with questions in his eyes. But all he could say was. "I'm watching you."

Asmodeus shrugged. "Watch all you want," he replied. "You won't see much."

Marcus looked at him for a second longer, then looked at Ben and Lucifer. "Come on," he said. "Let's go." They left the cement-like puddle on the floor and walked out the front door. Ben was the last one out, and took a long look at his house. He didn't know when the next time he would see it would be.

They walked down the familiar street towards Murphy's. Marcus looked uneasy, looking over his shoulder every four or five steps. "You looking for our friends?" Ben asked.

Marcus raised his eyebrows. "After all you've seen in the past few days, do you really think I'd be worried about a bunch of guys that pulled a fake sword on me? I have bigger issues on my mind at the minute," he replied.

"Of course, you do. That's why we're heading for Murphy's."

"Oh, shut up! I'm thirsty."

He walked on confidently. They walked up to the neon glowing entrance and stepped underneath it into the dimly lit bar. Marcus walked passed a few patrons sitting at the bar, two of them, elderly gentlemen drinking beer. One sitting, one standing. Mike was behind the bar, leaning on it, and had obviously been chatting with them. They noticed Marcus as he walked in and both gave him a wave. "How are ya, Marcus?" one of them asked.

"Hey Kev, Pat, Mike," Marcus said in greeting. "Doing well, thanks."

They both returned to their drinks, as Marcus headed over to his favourite stool and sat down. Ben saw Ryan at the pool table and beckoned for Azazel and Asmodeus to follow him over as he greeted Ryan. "Hey Marcus!" the bartender called over the music. "No knives today?"

"No Mike, not today. Give me the bad day scotch," he replied. The bartender pulled the blue colour labeled scotch down from the top shelf. Marcus had developed quite a taste for Johnnie Walker Blue. He had started with fine scotch, and moved his way up to what he believed was the finest. Even though it was still a blend, unlike other top shelf scotch, which were single malt, Marcus had his tastes. Mike poured Marcus his bad day scotch, with a single cube of ice, and sat the glass and the bottle down in front of him. He then glanced at Lucifer. "Luke!" he shouted. "I haven't seen you in here for years! How have you been?"

Marcus looked at Lucifer. He suddenly realised his brother had been checking up on him. "Just grab me another glass thanks Mike," he said. "I'll have what he's having." Mike grabbed a glass from underneath the bar. He side stepped to the ice tray, lifted the small metal scoop and shoveled the single ice cube into the glass. He sat the glass firmly on the bar in front of Lucifer, who then grabbed the blue labelled bottle and poured himself a dram. He picked it up and eyeballed the glass, then took a small swig. He grimaced at the taste. "I don't know how you can enjoy this stuff! It tastes like sulfur."

Marcus took a long sip of his drink and set it down on the bar. He rearranged it so that two sides of the hexagonal bottom of the glass were parallel with the bar. "The finest blends of scotch," he muttered. "There is nothing man made that is greater. It's like liquid silk."

"You need help!" Lucifer added.

Mike headed over to Pat and Kev to obviously continue a conversation they were having before Marcus and the others walked in. They looked over to the pool table where Ben was trying to teach Azazel how to play. Asmodeus was watching from a seat by the wall. "Tell me about the Ark then," Lucifer queried.

"Okay, well as I said." Marcus started, "you were given a riddle. The main reason for the riddle was a test. To see if you would tell me."

"That's not very nice," Lucifer interrupted.

Marcus looked at him. "You're not exactly a model angel," he continued. "Besides, how long has it been, now? Don't you think he'd be just a little bit skeptical?" Lucifer nodded.

"Anyway," Marcus kept going, "it was half right. We need to find a sacred box. The Ark of the Covenant was a symbol, just like the staff. We need to think closer to home. Think of a sacred chest that is within our grasp." Lucifer looked at the spirits on the wall behind the bar. First the bottom shelf, then the middle shelf, and then the expensive bottles that were on the top shelf. The answer hit him like lightning. "The chest in England. I mean the chest that Arus put there."

"Bingo!" Marcus said.

At that moment, Ben walked up to the bar to get drinks and heard the last of the conversation. "Why do you call him Arus, anyway? He's your father! Why don't you call him Dad?"

Lucifer and Marcus both looked at Ben like he was from another planet. Lucifer turned back to Marcus. "He has a point, you know," he said to Marcus

"Yeah," Ben added. "Get with the times!"

Mike came over to take Ben's order of drinks. "Uh, yes. I'll have three beers thanks, Mike."

"No worries, Ben," Mike replied. He grabbed three glasses from a rack next to the beer taps. The glasses looked like they had been in the fridge, as they were frosted before the beer was poured into them. Mike put the three glasses under the beer tap in a way that showed he had been doing this for many years. He left the beer tap running and filled the three glasses up one by one, without spilling a drop. He would just put the new glass in the old one's place. He placed the three beers on the bar in front of Ben. "You guys want this on your tabs?" he asked. Both Marcus and Ben nodded. Mike walked away to write up the tabs. Ben walked the three beers back over to Azazel and Asmodeus. He handed them out and took the last for himself. He raised the glass to them and went to drink it. Azazel and Asmodeus looked at each other and took a drink. They both spat the beer out in unison. "What do you call this?" Asmodeus asked.

"It's beer!" Ben replied. "Everybody drinks it. They say you're not a *man* unless you drink beer."

Ryan let out a small snorted laugh. They both looked down at the amber liquid. They tried another sip. "Takes a bit of getting used to." Azazel added. Ryan walked over to the bar next to Marcus, and leaned his elbows on it. "They let all kinds of people in this place," he said to Marcus.

"Ryan!" Marcus said. "Oh, I'd like you to meet my brother." Ryan stood upright and stared at Lucifer. He hesitantly put out his hand and Lucifer shook it. "Lucifer," Ryan said, "I'm honoured... and terrified." They finished shaking hands and Lucifer glanced at Marcus. "So, you know, then?"

Ryan nodded. "I knew something wasn't right about this guy the moment I met him. After many years of friendship, the truth came out. He's spoken of you, often. All good things I assure you." Lucifer smirked.

"I like this guy already. Why didn't you bring him instead of the kid?"

"Leave Ben alone," Marcus said. "Descendant of Amalie, remember?"

Lucifer sighed. "Yes, yes, I know. Family and all."

Ryan raised an eyebrow. "Family?"

"Long story," Marcus said.

Ryan nodded. "Fair enough. Well, it looks like you two are on official business," he said, as he looked at Lucifer. "What with you being on *earth* and all. So, I'll leave you to it." He tapped Marcus on the back. "Pleasure to meet you, Your Highness, Dark Lord, whatever I'm supposed to call you," Ryan said with a wave, as he turned to walk back to the pool table. Lucifer nodded.

"Oh, I like him a lot!" Lucifer said.

"Now now, don't let your head get any bigger."

Marcus and Lucifer watched him walk back to the pool table and checked to make sure Ben, Azazel and Asmodeus were getting along as they slowly subsided back into their conversation. "Where were we?" Lucifer asked.

"Chest in England."

"Right, so we have to go to England next," Lucifer stated.

"Pretty much," Marcus added. "But, I think we should be careful. I don't want any more nasty surprises like at Ben's house."

"I think that's just a little unavoidable. I mean, you, yourself said without a doubt, he'll send more."

"Oh, and he will. We just have to be a little more prepared," Marcus said, with his drink hovering in front of his lips. He took a sip, then gulped the last of it down. He placed the glass on the bar and rotated it again, to make the flat sides of the bottom parallel to the bar. He looked a question at Lucifer. "Do you think they're using possessions?"

Lucifer swatted his unfinished glass over to Marcus, who finished it in one gulp. "No, it can't be. Once again, it was only the five of us who knew we were going to Ben's house. And, unless someone or something was hiding in the shadows, I don't think any one of us had any time to tell anyone else, don't you?"

"Yeah, you have a point," Marcus said. He looked over his shoulder at the pool table.

"Should we trust them?" Lucifer asked.

Marcus kept staring. "We'll know soon enough," he said.

Chapter IV

They left Murphy's and headed back towards Marcus' apartment; walking north. They walked in the front door, up the elevator to the third floor and into the brown door with the number 23 on it. "You two, wait here." Marcus said. Azazel and Asmodeus waited outside the door. A cold breeze blew through the broken window from days before, and the place looked like it hadn't been touched since Marcus was last there. He threw his keys on the coffee table in the middle of the room, and walked into his bedroom. He made his way to the cupboard on the left of the doorway, opened it and stared. Marcus pulled out a chain necklace with a crucifix on it. He kissed it and held it to his chest. At the same time, he heard a noise from the ensuite. He quickly jerked his neck to the right towards the sound. He put the cross around his neck and closed the cupboard quietly.

Marcus walked past a lead pencilled 'X' in the wall and saw a faint glow coming from the bathroom. He stood next to the 'X' on the wall, which was only about two feet from the bathroom door. He kicked the door open and at the same time, put his fist through the 'X'. His hand came out with a golden, glowing short sword. He charged into the bathroom with the short sword held across his face and was blinded with a golden light. He fell to his knees and looked up at

Arus. His golden wings were open and the brightest Marcus had ever seen them. He had a brown coat on, with a grey shirt underneath, and old grey pants above dirty sneakers. He looked almost like a homeless man, with his long grey hair and beard. The short sword made a loud clanging sound on the tiles as it fell. Marcus opened his eyes wide. He couldn't see Arus' face due to the bright glow from the wings, but he knew it was him.

"I'm actually surprised that you didn't swing at me. I thought I'd be dead," Arus said.

Marcus got up off his knees. He brushed them off as if they almost hurt. "You're lucky you're not!" he replied. "What are you doing here?"

"I came to warn you. The company you travel with has some close ties with somebody you would rather not get involved with," Arus said.

"I already know that. I'm keeping an eye on them. The minute they slip up, they're gone. Besides, Lucifer is with us."

"Lucifer won't do a damn thing! And you know that!" Arus barked.

"Well, at least he's coming along for the ride. He could have very easily said no! What do you care anyway?"

"I care because you're both my family!" Arus bartered.

Marcus stared into his barely visible eyes. They glowed like fire. This is the angel that Marcus always wanted to be. He always followed in his footsteps; killing demons from a very young age, behind his father's back. The time they spent together during their exile from Heaven, was where they spent a lot of time researching many things, gaining knowledge that others would be dumbfounded by. But, Arus knew Marcus would always grow to be a mighty warrior. He'd heard some say that Marcus would become the best. But, Arus didn't speak to many others nowadays. He never really got the chance to, unless they were bound to earth just like he and Marcus were.

"Go find your sword, son," Arus said, "and take the position that was once mine, and now belongs to you."

Marcus played with the cross dangling just below his neck. His father stood back and gave him some room. Lucifer burst in with his sword ready. "What's all the noise about?" he shouted, as he saw the glowing figure in front of Marcus. "Dad!" he cried. "What are you doing here?"

"Dad?" Arus remarked. Marcus looked at Lucifer as if to say *You actually listened to Ben?* Lucifer looked at Marcus and Arus in turn, although looking at Arus almost blinded him as he was glowing a bright gold. He put an arm up in front of his eyes. "Shut up!" he said to both of them.

"Well, I must leave," Arus said.

"Leave?" Lucifer questioned. "You just got here. Where are you going?"

"Back to his little cave," Marcus sighed.

"I'm sorry boys, it's the only place for me now."

He vanished. Lucifer picked up the golden sword on the floor. He looked at it and handed it back to Marcus. "What did he tell you?" Lucifer asked.

"Nothing much, as always," Marcus replied.

"Seems to be the norm, lately," Lucifer remarked.

Marcus walked out of the bathroom and stood next to the broken wall. He pulled a little piece of plaster off and inspected it. He crumbled it in his hand and dropped the remains. He wandered through his bedroom, back towards the cupboard, and opened it and stared inside for a long moment. Something was in there, that wasn't before. Something he recognised from somewhere in his past. It was round, thick and silver, with a small gap to fit over your wrist. A cuff. It had the same tribal etchings on it as the ring Marcus wore around his thumb. Marcus knew exactly what it was, and who put it there. And now he knew exactly what was in the chest in the Chislehurst caves in England. He put the cuff on and the gap closed up, like he knew it would. It was as if the metal stretched to join the gap together. Lucifer looked over his shoulder with awe.

"That's what's in the chest, isn't it?" he asked. "The battle commander's effects."

Marcus nodded. "Except for this. He kept it on him. Just to be safe, in case somebody came across the chest. The pieces are useless, unless they're all together." Marcus pulled his jacket down over the cuff and closed the cupboard door. He and Lucifer walked out into the lounge room. "Okay, we're good to go," Marcus said.

"Where to?" Ben asked.

"Chislehurst, in England," he replied. He grabbed his keys off the table, looked out the broken window to the street and headed for the front door. Marcus locked the door from the outside, walked up to Ben and grabbed him by the arm as the others all put a hand on him, so they transported all together. The room disappeared around them slowly, and they were suddenly standing in a small street, surrounded by buildings. They all looked around to inspect their new surroundings. It was early morning as there was a slight fog, and Ben was shivering. "Why is it so cold here?" he asked.

"It's not," Marcus said. "It's 6am. It's like this in the US in the mornings as well. You're just never awake to witness it."

"Oh, shut up!" Ben remarked. "Where are we?"

Marcus walked towards what looked like a main street at the end of the small street. He turned and looked at the other end of the street, and then looked at Lucifer. "Don't ask me," Lucifer said. "I've never been here before."

Marcus gave him a look that almost said, *Well, what good are you?* He walked up to the main street and looked around. Across the road, he saw a bunch of trees on the roadside and a pond beyond the trees. He saw a bus stop neatly sheltered by the trees. He looked left down the main road. It was very quiet, and there was only a few cars about. He looked up at the street sign leading into the small street he came out of. *Camden Grove.* He looked back at the main road and turned to walk back to the others. "We're in Chislehurst," he said. "But, we're nowhere near the caves. We'll have to walk from here."

"Why can't we just transport there?" Ben asked.

"Geez, this kid asks a lot of questions," Lucifer said. "We risk exposure if we transport. We'll have to walk from here, because this is a secluded location. It's safe to transport here."

Marcus started walking towards the main road, beckoning the rest of them to follow him. "From memory, it's only about half an hour, to an hour's walk. Won't be too long," he said as he walked.

"But, how long has it been since you walked there from here?" Lucifer asked.

"Since before that golf course was ever there. I used to be able to walk straight through there," Marcus replied. "Now, let's go."

They started walking south down Chislehurst High Street and turned right into Prince Imperial Road at a strange lop sided, 'X' shaped intersection. Prince Imperial Road ran alongside the Chislehurst Common. Marcus looked to his left at the common. He started to picture Eden in his head. He remembered being told about a war memorial on the other side of Chislehurst Common with a large sword on it. He wanted to go and look at it, just to bring him closer to the idea that he would have his sword back very soon. *I'll check it out later,* he thought. The day was brightening up and people were emerging from the woods surrounding them. People were going for their morning jogs, or walking their dogs. The road cut through the common and now trees were on both sides of them. They continued walking. "What did he do here, anyway?" Lucifer asked.

"That's all very cloak and dagger. He doesn't talk much about it," Marcus replied. "He fought, and he met Amalie. I guess once that was found out, he buried the chest in the caves, and kept one of the cuffs himself."

"We're looking for a buried chest in a cave? How quaint," Asmodeus mocked.

"What?" Marcus asked.

"Well, we're not exactly pirates, are we? Looking for buried treasure, there's talk of getting a boat. What next?"

"I'll make you walk the plank next!" Marcus muttered.

Asmodeus stared at him and then focused on where his feet were going. They came to a small junction with about four other streets leading off, and a large cricket ground to the left. They turned right onto Old Hill. Lucifer looked at Marcus. "You sure you know where you're going? Or are you just wandering?"

"It's this way. Trust me," Marcus said, as he kept walking. They walked past parked cars and houses, and people walking out on the street. They looked like a small gang, a little out of place. Marcus and Ben were the only two that actually looked like they blended in. Marcus' jacket was very European style. They came up to Caveside Close. "Ahh, here we are!" Marcus said. They walked down to the end of Caveside Close until they came up to the Caves Entrance building. It was a long structure with a gift shop, and the entrance to the cave was off to the side. The doors were closed and locked. They walked up to the doors and tried to open them. "Help you?" a voice said from behind.

They all turned around. There was a middle-aged man leaning on a post by the gift shop door, looking at the five of them. "We're trying to get into the caves," Ben said. Marcus hit him on the back of the head.

"What he means to say, is we would like to have a look inside the caves." The man pursed his lips and shifted his mouth to the side, as he looked them all up and down. "Tours start from 10am," he said.

Marcus breathed a laugh out through his nose. "What we need, can't be shown by any tour guide," he said.

"And what do you supposed that would be?" the man questioned.

"A chest," Ben replied.

"A chest? Well I've not seen any chests in there," the man said.

Marcus looked at Ben. "I'll handle this, Ben," he said as he stepped to the front of the group. "What do you know about Hebrew?"

"Absolutely nothing, why?"

"Okay, how many times have you been through the caves?" Marcus asked.

The man looked Marcus up and down again. Marcus grew tired of his eyeballing. "How many days have you lived?"

Now Marcus was getting impatient. "Okay, out of all the days that you've been in the cave, and out of all the inscriptions on the wall, have you ever come across four letters on a wall at about eye level, that look like they were written about eight hundred years ago, in what looks like a foreign alphabet?"

The man pushed himself off the post he was leaning on with intrigue in his eyes. "What do you know about it?" he asked.

"Well, I know that its pronounced ARON, and that it sometimes glows. Now, what do *you* know about it?" Marcus asked.

"I know they're there. Never thought anything of it."

"But, you know enough to know that somebody would one day ask about it," Marcus questioned.

The man nodded. "He was here last night. He said you'd come."

"Who?" Lucifer asked.

"The big old fella. Told me to make sure you boys got in and nobody else," the man replied.

"What did he look like? What did he call himself?" Lucifer persisted.

"Well, funnily enough he called himself Aron. He said I'd know it was you because one of you would say his name; whereas, anybody else wouldn't have." He looked at Marcus as he spoke. "So, you must be Marcus."

Marcus looked at Ben and Lucifer. "Yes, I am," he said.

"I'm James, I'll go get the keys."

James went to get the keys. Ben and Lucifer looked at Marcus. "Who's Aron?" they both asked at the same time.

Marcus rolled his eyes. "It's Arus. He called himself Aron because that's what the inscription on the wall says. He knew I'd say it, so he called himself Aron and said I'd mention his name," Marcus replied.

Both Ben and Lucifer nodded in agreement. "Smart guy," Ben said. James came out with the keys and walked up to the doors. He unlocked them and opened them up. They all walked inside and James locked the door from the inside. He grabbed a lantern and led them down the large steps, holding onto the rail in the middle as he went. They went down the steps and found themselves in a large opening, which James referred to as the entrance. "We don't usually do this, but the fella was very persistent. This way," he said.

He led them through twists and turns of tunnels and passageways. The cave was very dark, and only the light from the lantern could be seen. They started hearing noises. Marcus stopped and his sword appeared in his hand. James turned around to see what they were doing, and saw the swords. "What are you doing?" he asked.

"I heard something," Marcus said.

"Well, of course you did. These caves are haunted. I'm sure you'll run into many ghosties and ghoulies down here," James said, as he turned around to keep walking.

"It's not ghosties and ghoulies I'm worried about," Marcus added.

James continued to walk through the passageways in front of them. They passed what looked like an old war hospital with mannequins just inside. They kept walking. "How far is it?" Azazel asked.

"There is about thirty-five kilometres of caves down here. You thought it would be in the first *one*?" James asked. Marcus had warmed up to James. He was so openly blunt; no matter whether it insulted somebody. A man like that could make anybody feel stupid, even over the simplest thing. Marcus noticed a glowing coming from behind him, as well as from the lantern in front of him. He turned around to see Ben's pendant glowing. At that moment, a dark figure moved quickly in front of James. Everyone stepped back. Marcus pulled his sword up, ready to strike. James turned around. "Didn't I say you'll run into ghosties down here?" he asked with a smirk.

They all heard a snarling sound; loud, clear and close. "That ain't no ghosty," Marcus said.

"That was quite louder than normal," James said.

There was a loud screeching, roaring sound right next to them. Marcus grabbed the pendant around Ben's neck and pulled it off. He held it high in the air. The chain dangled out of his closed fist. "Light!" he yelled. The pendant lit up a furious white light that burned the whole passageway. The demon stood in front of them, shielding its eyes and snarling. It looked just like the demon that attacked them at Ben's house. Marcus noticed Asmodeus step back a little. He ran to the demon and swirled his sword around his head, while holding the pendant out with his left. He swung at the demon and sliced its head clean off. The head fell to the floor and turned into the same wet muddy cement-like liquid as before. The body did the same. Marcus stood upright and dangled the pendant in front of his face. He blew at it and the light died back down to a glow. He handed it back to Ben. "How did you do that?" Ben asked, as he fastened it back around his neck.

"I told you, I made it," Marcus replied.

James composed himself and turned back to walk in front, and stepped back with a gasp as he bumped into a dark figure that disappeared instantly. "You see?" he said, "ghosties and ghoulies." It was as if he was unfazed by the demon they'd just killed. He continued down the passageway. Ben's pendant started glowing a little brighter. "We're getting close," Marcus said.

"Right you are, Marcus," James said. "Here it is."

They stopped and walked over to the wall. There was a word written in Hebrew on the wall.

ארון

They all stared at the word. It was glowing furiously, just as Ben's pendant was. "That's the brightest I've ever seen it," James said. "What does it say?"

"It's pronounced ARON. It's Hebrew." Marcus ran his fingers along it as he spoke. He turned to the others. "It means ARK." Lucifer looked at him in disbelief, as Marcus stepped back to let the others inspect it. "This is getting too quizzical for me," Lucifer sighed.

"So how do we get in?" Ben asked, trying to push the wall. "Wait, what do you mean get in?" James asked.

At that moment, Marcus rushed at the wall and burst through it with his shoulder. He fell on the ground, on top of the rubble he just blasted through. He wiped all the dirt and dust from his face. He stood up and dusted himself off. He looked around the small room. It had a very low roof, and was only about ten square feet. There was a small chest at the far end of the room. Everyone crowded in behind him. "This is like something out of Indiana Jones," James said. "Any minute now, big circular saws are gonna come chop our heads off!" he said, waving his arms. Everyone turned and stared at him. "What?" he asked, innocently.

Marcus walked up to the chest and knelt down in front of it. As he reached out to open it, his jacket sleeve receded a little and he noticed that the cuff around his wrist gave off its very own small glow. He opened the chest. A bright glow came from inside the chest. Marcus focused his eyes and saw what he knew he would see. He picked up the other cuff and settled it on his left wrist. The cuff was the same as the one he found in his cupboard. The gap closed quickly the same as the old one. He had both the cuffs on his wrists, and they both had a faint glow.

There was also a platinum belt in the chest. Marcus picked it up and looked at it with a reminiscent thought. He had seen Arus wear it a long time ago. It was more like a platinum cummerbund, with a sharp point that stuck up above the stomach. He undid his own belt buckle and yanked it through all the hoops in his jeans, and then lifted up his jacket and shirt to clasp the platinum belt around his waist. The glow from the cuffs got a little brighter. He inspected the belt around his waist, and as he was looking down, he noticed something else shining in the chest. He reached in and pulled out a ring. It was silver and wide, and identical to the ring on his right thumb, only a few sizes smaller. He put in on the third finger of his right hand. He looked at his hand - first at the palm, then at the back, then back to the palm. He inspected how the ring looked next to its twin. He clenched his fist and grabbed his sword, stood up and turned around to face everybody. He held the sword with a ready stance.

Everybody stared at Marcus, wondering what he was doing, except for James who was snarling and ripping bits of skin off his face. His face was bloody and the skin was stretching as he was pulling on it, revealing a gruesome bloody mess underneath. Everybody turned to look at James and saw him turning into a demon, as more bits of skin and flesh were torn away. They all took a step back. Ben pulled his bow staff, and Lucifer drew his sword. "This one's mine!" Lucifer shouted.

The demon came forward, swiping at them. It swiped a fast arm at Lucifer who sliced its arm off with a quick dash of his sword. The demon's arm grew back almost instantly. They all stood back. Lucifer backed up to Marcus. "Did you know they could do that?" he asked Marcus, while still staring at the demon.

"No, I didn't. In fact, I'm pretty sure they can't," Marcus replied.

Marcus walked up to the demon with a very confident walk. He put his sword behind his head like a baseball player and sliced the demons head clean off. The head toppled to the floor and the body just stayed there. Something started growing out of its neck. Within a few seconds, the growth was fully formed into a head. "That's not a demon," Marcus said. "You might want to get out of here."

Marcus stood there with his sword ready, and the others didn't move. "I said get out of here!" he shouted. They all ran around the demon and out of the hole in the wall. Marcus stayed in the room to hold off the demon. "What the hell is that thing, then?" Ben asked.

"I think it's Baal," Lucifer replied.

"What the hell is Baal?" Ben screamed.

"Baal is a devil. He is basically second in charge in Purgatory," Lucifer said.

"Oh, great!" Ben said.

Marcus stared into the demon's eyes. He put his sword away, and stood front on to the demon. "This is what you want, isn't it Baal? No weapons? Marcus asked. Baal nodded.

"Well, come on then," Marcus said. "Show yourself." Horns started growing out of the demon's head, and curled around, almost like a merino sheep. More horns started emerging from its spine. The body grew in size, and a tail formed itself, with large spikes on it. Marcus waited impatiently for the transformation. Baal couldn't stand upright in the room. He glared at Marcus with his fiery eyes and was almost growling with every breath. "He sent others after you, but I figured this is something I should take care of myself," Baal growled.

"So, he thinks you'd fuck it up, and decided to send someone who could get the job done. I can see how you'd be anxious to prove him wrong. Allow me to prove him right," Marcus smirked.

Baal roared. It echoed through the entire cave. The others heard it and Lucifer went running back to the hole in the wall. He saw Baal standing there with his back to him. "Oh shit!" he said. Baal turned around and saw Lucifer. His tail almost whipped Marcus as he turned. He roared again and bent down to a crouch. Fire shot out of his mouth and Lucifer jumped out of the way just as the flames burst through the hole. Baal felt something on his tail, he tried to turn but his tail was pinned. He glanced over his shoulder at his tail and saw Marcus standing on it. "Don't get distracted now," Marcus said.

Marcus jumped off the tail and opened his wings. He lunged forward like a bullet and tackled Baal. The impact thrust Baal backward and through the hole in the wall. Marcus was still holding onto him and they both crashed into the wall opposite the hole. The others watched in disbelief as Marcus and Baal wrestled. Marcus plunged his fists into the reptile-like body. Left, right, left, like it was a punching bag. Baal was letting out gasps of pain. Marcus had worked his way on top of Baal and began to uppercut his chin with every punch. Just small uppercuts, winding his arm with each strike. They were impressive blows, and they were certainly doing damage. Ben watched in awe. He had seen Marcus fight many times, but never like this. It seemed that fighting demons needed a superhuman fighting style. Ben was amazed, watching like a coach watches a boxer, mimicking the moves throughout the fight. But, Ben was learning. He always had a knack for being able to watch something and almost replicate it. He figured this style would be useful for his future in becoming an angel. Might help on earth too.

Baal finally grabbed a hold of Marcus and threw him off. He crashed against the wall near Lucifer. "Ben, the pendant!" he shouted. Ben pulled the pendant off his neck and threw it to Marcus, who fastened it around his own neck. He launched himself at Baal again, landing on his back and avoiding the spikes. He grabbed hold of Baal's two curled horns on the top of his head, and jerked his head to the left, and then to the right in a quick move. Baals neck snapped with a loud crack that echoed for seconds afterwards. His body went limp and he fell to the ground, with Marcus still on his back. Once he hit the ground, he burst into a muddy puddle, and Marcus fell face first into it. He got up and wiped the grey liquid from his eyes and flicked it at the floor. The pendant was glowing brightly. They had no lantern anymore, and the only light they had was from the pendant, but it was bright enough. There was silence while Marcus tried to clean himself off with his hands. The others all started laughing. "What's so funny?" Marcus asked.

"I think you're going to need a shower, and you'll need to wash your clothes," Ben said. Marcus looked at his body covered with the grey muddy liquid. He walked up to Ben and place both hands on his shoulders, then tackled him into the puddle. "Now you do too," he laughed. Ben got up and wiped as much off as he could. "Now, let's find some water, and keep a look out. Arus might have left something else down here," Marcus said.

They walked through the caves, trying to see if Arus may have left anything else in there. Azazel walked up to Marcus and tapped him on the shoulder. "Very impressive back there, boyo!" he said. Marcus wasn't fond of the way he spoke. He used the letter 'v' instead of 'th' so *there* sounded like *vere*. "Thanks," Marcus said.

They wandered through the depths of the caves, hoping to find some sort of sign that there may be something more there. "I'm getting the feeling that we are being followed, but not in the entirety of the word," Marcus said. "It seems like somebody knows our moves and is alerting someone else about it. But who?"

"It would have to be somebody with friends in high places," Lucifer added.

"I agree," Marcus replied. "They sent Baal after us. He's not going to be happy next time he sees me."

"Wait," Ben said. "I thought he was dead now."

"Oh no, he's just not on earth anymore," Marcus clarified.

"Oh, so we'll be seeing him again then?" Ben asked.

"Without a doubt," Marcus said.

They walked a bit further through the caves. "Who could it be?" Marcus asked.

"I'm sure we'll find out soon," Lucifer said.

Eventually, they gave up looking for something, and tried to find the exit through the maze. "You know, I think James locked it from the inside," Ben said.

"Well we can't walk out then," Marcus added.

Marcus heard a sound. It was a sound he had heard before and the hairs on the back of his neck stood up. He closed his eyes to concentrate, to make sure he was really hearing it. "So, what do we do?" Ben asked.

"Shh!" Marcus emphatically whispered.

They all stopped and listened. Marcus heard it again. It was a stone grinding on metal sound; very short, but very distinct.

Shunk...

Marcus let out a breath through his nose. "Shit," he said.

"What?" Lucifer asked, "What is it?"
Shunk...

"I think I know that sound," Azazel said.

Marcus nodded. "Get Ben out of here. Right now!" Marcus said.

"Will someone please tell me what the hell is going on?" Ben asked.

Shunk...

It was louder that time, and definitely coming from behind them.

"Just go, run, that way! As fast as you can. Do not come back for me." They began running as Marcus readied himself. His blue wings rose up out of his back, and he put his hands together and closed his eyes. He knew he was in for a big fight.

SHUNK...

The sound was right behind him as Marcus feinted left. The dagger swiped right where he was just standing, as Orias came into view. He swiped again as Marcus ducked and feinted away again. He feinted right and his head was met with the large stone in Orias' left hand, as he staggered to his left. He fell into a quick roll as the dagger swiped at him again. A hand appeared out of nowhere and thrust him against the wall. Eligos came into view as Marcus complied. He stayed against the wall as Orias stood triumphantly behind Eligos. He crossed his arms with his dagger hanging out of his hand, and the large stone still in his left.

"My dear Marcus," Eligos seductively said. "It's been far too long." Marcus was silent. She wiped some of the grey pasty liquid off his jacket and inspected it closely, then licked it off her finger as she looked at Marcus. She closed her eyes and moaned slightly. "Mmm, Baal," she said, "I'm almost impressed." Marcus struggled a little as she tightened her grip. "That wouldn't be wise, my dear boy. You know what happens if you kill me. We wouldn't want you becoming the Archfiend, now would we? Taking on the throne, Beelzebub's successor." Marcus stopped his struggle and stared at her in anger. "It's funny, you know. Everyone only talks about Arthur and Lancelot. They don't discuss Merlin and his love child with a human. They talk of him as a wizard! Yet, he was the one who created the Nephilim. With my help, of course.

"Yes, I know," Marcus said, "Morgan Le Fay."

"Now there's a name I haven't heard in some time. You're a clever little boy, aren't you?" Eligos licked Marcus' cheek. He squirmed in disgust. "Aw, don't be so delicate. Time to go night, night."

Orias rushed forward with his left hand outstretched beside him; the stone was coming fast towards Marcus' head, and he needed to quicken his thinking. He used all his strength to shoot upward as far as possible against Eligos' strong hand around his neck. He luckily got up far enough, and fast enough that the colossal blow from the stone hit Eligos in the hand instead. She lost her grip on Marcus' neck as he slipped sideways behind her, and his right elbow came up as he wrapped his left hand around his right fist and thrust his elbow into the back of Eligos' head. She staggered forward and turned around, as the two of them advanced on Marcus. He kept walking backwards until he found himself up against another wall. Orias and Eligos pounced and began hitting him, hard and fast. He held his arms up to cover his face as they kept coming. His anger boiled more and more, as the Amulet of the Shadows around his neck began to glow furiously. Marcus held his arms out by his side and erupted in a flash of light that thrust Orias and Eligos backwards. They were temporarily blinded from the flash, as they staggered and regained their vision. Marcus was gone.

Ben was surrounded by trees. He looked around him and could see water through a gap in the trees. Lucifer, Azazel and Asmodeus weren't there. He walked towards the water and kept looking around. "Lucifer?" he called. He reached into his pockets and pulled out his mobile phone and his wallet, and dumped them on the sand. He looked around and couldn't see anybody. He walked into the water and dove under to wash off the grey cement-like liquid. He resurfaced and looked to the beach to see if his phone and wallet were okay. There was a man going through his wallet. "Hey!" he yelled out. The man looked up and saw Ben in the water. He looked left and right, and picked up the phone and started to run. He stopped immediately. A hand was around his neck and hoisting him up in the air. The man dropped Ben's phone and wallet, and tried to see who was hoisting him up. "Well, I'll no doubt be seeing *you* again," Lucifer said from beside Azazel.

Azazel tightened his grip on the man's neck and then dropped him. The man ran. Lucifer picked up Ben's wallet and phone, and held them up in the air. Ben put his hand out of the water and waved a thank you gesture. He got out of the water and walked up onto the beach to where Lucifer, Azazel and Asmodeus were. "Thanks," Ben said to Lucifer and Azazel.

"Don't mention it," Lucifer said.

Ben fought to dry himself off and looked around. "Where's Marcus?" Ben asked.

Lucifer pondered. "Couldn't tell you. You should know, where does he go after a fight?"

"That's providing he won," Azazel said.

"Come now," Lucifer remarked. "Marcus is a lot tougher than you think."

Azazel shifted his head from side to side in a half agreeing manner. "Yes, well, after seeing him take on Baal, I've got a lot more respect for him. But, I remember what that sound was we heard in the cave that got him so unsettled. It was Orias."

Lucifer tilted his head to the side. "As in, Orias and Eligos?"

Azazel nodded. "Even I'm not dumb enough to fight them."

"No," Lucifer added, "nor is Marcus. He knows that..."

Lucifer looked at Ben. "Well, he just knows he shouldn't."

"If it's something that would annoy him, he'd be at home."

"Well then, let's go there."

Lucifer grabbed Ben on the shoulder as Azazel and Asmodeus put their hands on Lucifer's shoulder. They were all instantly standing outside Marcus' apartment door. Ben checked the handle and found the door was unlocked. He opened it and peered in. "Marcus? It's Ben. We're coming in." Ben and Lucifer walked past the crosses in the entrance way and into the apartment. "I still don't understand how those crosses don't harm you," Ben said.

Lucifer scoffed. "Hello, my name's Lucifer," he stated sarcastically.

"Right," Ben said.

Ben looked around a bit and walked through the apartment. He went to the left towards the bedroom, and heard the shower running in the ensuite. He walked to the door and knocked. "Marcus, it's Ben. You alright?" There was no response.

Ben built up the courage to open the door and saw a fully clothed figure in the shower. He opened the shower door and saw Marcus, soaked to the skin and blood being washed away down the drain. "Holy shit! You okay, man?"

"I'm fine."

Lucifer walked in. "It went that well, huh?"

Lucifer held his hand up to Marcus' face as a small glow came from it. It healed the wounds on Marcus' face and Marcus stepped out of the shower. "Oh, I gotta learn how to do that!" Ben said.

"What happened?" Lucifer asked.

"I got away," Marcus said. "Don't worry, I didn't kill her."

"Good. Let's try to avoid them as best we can, okay?"

Ben's thoughts started racing. "Why are you so scared of them?"

"We're not," Marcus said. "It's just best we avoid them. Eligos is a succubus, and Orias is an Incubus. He's not that much of a threat to us, although he hits like a truck. But, if she gets close enough to work her seduction on you, you're as good as dead."

"Okay," Ben said. "That makes sense. Keeping our distance then."

"Avoiding like the plague."

"So, now what?" Lucifer asked. "We have the staff, we have the trinkets. Shall we go get it?"

Marcus dried himself off with a towel as best as he could; ruffling it through his hair, which gave it a natural curl. "Not yet," Marcus said. "I think we need to find out how they're getting to us. We need information. It's almost as if we're going in blind, and they're throwing everything they've got at us. We need to know where they're getting their intel."

"So, what do you suggest?"

Marcus smirked. "Samael."

* * *

"So, you decided to take it upon yourself to interfere. And look what happened. I told you they had it under control,"

Beelzebub said. He was standing on the stairs leading up to his archaic throne, looking down at Baal. He had been returned to the lair upon his arrival back to Purgatory with his death. Beelzebub was not impressed. "Now, what do I do with you? Do I relieve you of your duty? Do I send you back into battle?"

"Do what you must, sire," Baal responded.

The devil nodded his large, scaly head. The shrouded figure entered from Purgatory as Beelzebub looked up. The figure almost stopped at the site of Baal on his knees, and seemed to pause with a little hesitation. "News?" Beelzebub asked.

"Marcus escaped from Orias and Eligos."

Baal stood up, with a newfound sense of hope. "We should send an army," he said.

"No..." Beelzebub cut in. "Send a human, and call the authorities."

"What will that prove?" The figure asked.

"If he is seen killing by law enforcement, he'll be put in prison. We can get to him there. Do we know where they are now?"

"I believe they are heading to see Samael."

The devil looked at Baal. "Maybe there's use for you, yet." His hands lit up with fire, as his hand moved forward and pierced Baal's chest with his large talons. A fatal move to an enemy, but to his own kin, a rather powerful force. Baal's evil power resurged within him.

* * *

"I haven't seen Sam in years," Lucifer said. "How's he doing?"

"He's hiding," Marcus said. "Sure enough, over the years, he pissed off one too many angels and demons by switching sides, that he had to go underground. But, he still knows everything. He'll know who's after us."

They were standing in what looked like an alley way, behind a row of houses. On one side of the alley were wooden fences; on the other side was a hill that merged into a large, open green marsh. They walked to the end of the alley, and around to the front of the houses. They walked through the gate of the third house and up to the front door. Marcus knocked on the door. It opened about two inches and stopped abruptly against the chain. Marcus saw an eye peeking out at him, then it disappeared. "It's Marcus and Lucifer," the voice whispered. Marcus heard talking inside, but couldn't pick up on what they were saying. The eye came back to the crack in the door. "Are you armed?" the voice asked.

"Of course, I am. Let me the hell in!" Marcus demanded. He heard a faint, *let him in* through the crack. The door almost closed and Marcus could hear the chain rattling. The door opened fully, and a short overweight man stood in the doorway with his hand on the handle. Marcus stepped in, Lucifer followed, then Ben, Azazel, and Asmodeus last. "Marcus! Lucifer! To what do I owe the pleasure?" Sam asked.

He was sitting on a filthy couch at the far end of the room, rolling what Marcus pretended to believe was a cigarette over a glass coffee table. He was quite small and tanned, and had thick black hair on his head. He was wearing a blue singlet and big baggy jeans, and big black boots. The room had a deep smoky haze, hovering at about eye level. There were three others in the room; one on the couch with Sam leaving a gap in between them, one sitting on an armchair that ran at a right angle to the couch the other two were sitting on, and opposite an empty arm chair just like it on the other side of the coffee table, and the short overweight man who was now closing the door behind Asmodeus. "This isn't exactly a social visit, Sam," Lucifer said.

"Wait," Sam replied. "Let me guess. You want seasonal tickets to the Yankees!" Samael and his three companions laughed. Marcus walked up to the couch in between the coffee table and the empty armchair next to it. He put his boot onto Sam's knee and pushed down on it. Sam gasped in pain and straightened his leg. Big mistake. Marcus put a little more pressure on it.

"I think you're enjoying your stay here a little too much, Sam. We can always send you home," he said. He took his foot off of Sam's leg and sat down in the armchair.

"There ain't no way I'm going back there!" Sam stated. "What do you want?"

"I just got a visit," Marcus said, looking at his fingernails. "From Baal, Orias and Eligos. You wouldn't know anything about that would you?"

"Why would I? I don't hang around in those circles anymore. You know that."

Marcus nodded. He did know that. "That's very true," he said. "But, you have friends who do, don't you?"

"I got friends just like anybody else, but they don't tell me much, and I don't ask. You know what I'm saying?"

Marcus stared at him for a long second. "No, I don't," he said. He stood up and put his boot back on Sam's knee.

"Okay, they do tell me!" Sam shouted. Marcus sat down again.

"So, what do they tell you?" he asked.

Samael looked around the room at his friends, and at the four that walked in with Marcus. "Don't even think about trying something. There's five of us and four of you, and you know it'll be over before my friends even join in."

Sam nodded. "Okay, word is that you two are looking for your sword, and apparently you've figured out that it's the one at the garden, but you don't know how to get there. So, you're digging up stuff to help you along the way," he said.

"Who told you this?" Marcus asked.

"I told you, my friends hang in those circles. They give me bits and pieces. They mentioned that there's a snitch. Somebody who knows everything you're doing and relaying it back to Beelzebub."

"Beelzebub? Ben asked. "I thought that was you!" He pointed to Lucifer.

"Ahh, another apprentice I see!" Sam said. "You got a good teacher, kid!" he yelled to Ben.

"Yes, so everyone keeps telling me. So, who the hell is Beelzebub then?"

"The devil," Marcus said.

"But that's..." He stopped speaking with his hand halfway towards pointing at Lucifer again. "Okay, I'm confused," he finished.

"Beelzebub is the devil. He is treacherous, murderous, and ugly!" Lucifer said. "Me, I just punish the wicked."

"I'm never gonna get this," Ben said.

"Forget about it!" Marcus yelled. "Who's the snitch?"

"I don't know, but it's someone very close. Someone who doesn't know the consequences."

"Consequences?" Asmodeus asked. "What consequences?"

Marcus looked sideways at Asmodeus. His thoughts started racing. Samael smirked. "Yes, consequences," he said. "Whoever he is, he doesn't know about the power of the sword and what it could do. You all better realise, Marcus is the only one that can touch the sword. This thing was created to eliminate demons, and that's exactly what it will do." Marcus looked over at Azazel and Asmodeus. He nodded and looked at Sam. "Thanks Sam. I appreciate it," he said.

They stood up and shook hands. "You know I'll help where I can.," Sam said.

"Thank you. By the way, do you have a phone?" Marcus asked.

"Yeah, why?" Sam asked.

"Ben, write down your number and give it to Sam," Marcus instructed.

Ben looked around at Lucifer, then Sam, then Marcus. "Why?" he asked.

"So, he can call us if he gets any information," Marcus replied.

Ben shrugged and walked over to the coffee table where there was pen and paper. He wrote his and Marcus' names on the paper, and his phone number below them. He pulled his phone out of his pocket and handed it to Marcus. "What do I need it for?" Marcus asked.

"Well, he's going to be calling you," Ben replied. "And, it's not like anybody calls me on it anyway."

"Okay," Marcus said. "Sam, call us if you hear anything."

"I will, Marcus. Vaya con Dios."

Marcus looked sternly at Sam. "I plan to." Marcus walked to the front door and let himself out. The others followed him. They walked out the front gate and turned left to go around the back to the alley. "He just said 'Go with God' in Spanish and I understood it... I don't speak Spanish," Ben said.

"Angels speak a universal language. We understand it all as if everyone were speaking the same. What happened at the Tower of Babel just cloaked the universal language so that the humans could not understand each other," Marcus replied.

"So, that really happened? And that's why there are different languages?"

"Yep."

"So, why is Sam so afraid of you?" Ben asked.

"Because I know where he lives," Marcus said, as he stopped dead in the middle of the alley way. Lucifer bumped into him.

"Why did you stop?" Lucifer asked, as he followed Marcus' gaze to the entrance of the alley. There was a man standing there, looking directly at them, waiting for them. Marcus put up his hand to make the others stay back. He calmly started walking up to the man. He had his hand behind his back as he walked. He tilted his hand up underneath his jacket and pulled out his sword. He quickly pulled it around to his front and swung at the man. A sword appeared in the man's hand. He blocked Marcus' swing. Marcus stepped back and tried to swing again with both hands from the left. The man quickly blocked. Marcus had fought many sword fights, and never had a scratch on him. He smiled a quick smile and spun around in a complete circle. He swung the sword out as he spun and also ducked. The man tried to strike at Marcus' head, but missed by two feet. Marcus' sword hit the man's leg. The man fell, still trying to swing his sword at Marcus, but Marcus just dodged him and drove his sword right through the man's chest. The man clutched his chest in pain and breathed one last breath. His head crashed onto the ground below him.

"Freeze!" Marcus heard from behind him, along with the familiar click of automatic weapons. He turned around to see two police officers pointing guns at him. He put his sword back up under his jacket and put his hands in the air.

"Drop the weapon!" one of them shouted.

"It's gone!" Marcus shouted back.

"No, drop it!" the officer yelled back.

"You'll have to come and get it," Marcus said.

The officers moved in closer to him, holding their guns out straight. These two had had a lot of practise; covering him from a wide angle. Their guns were pointed slightly behind Marcus, to make up for alignment if he ran. Marcus knew bullets wouldn't harm him, but he didn't want them to know that. He still had his arms half up. One officer holstered his gun and pulled out a set of handcuffs. He grabbed Marcus' arms and cuffed them both behind his back. The other officer covered Marcus with the gun. The officer that cuffed Marcus patted him up and down. "The sword is gone. I can't find it anywhere," he said.

"Just put him in the car. We'll strip search him at the station," the other officer said. They grabbed an arm each, and led Marcus over to the car. The officer that cuffed him started reading Marcus his rights. Marcus looked over to his shoulder and yelled to the others. "Go to Ben's' house. I'll meet you there."

"No, you won't," one of the officers said. They put him in the back of the police car. His cuffed wrists pulled his shoulders back. He shuffled his backside forward to get comfortable for the ride, and sat in silence. One of the police officers opened the driver's side door and called in the details of what just happened on the radio. The radio burst back in his ear with a loud, distorted tone. He pulled a lever down beside the driver's seat and the boot latch clicked. The other officer walked around to the boot and opened it up. He slammed it down shut and had a large roll of yellow tape in his hands. He walked over to the man lying on the street, and checked for a pulse. He looked up at the other officer and shook his head, and then started taping off the area. An ambulance arrived and began to check the body. After a few checks, they put a white sheet over it. The officers got in the front and sat there. The officer that cuffed him was in the passenger seat, turned around to keep an eye on him. "How could you do that? In broad daylight, in the middle of the street?" he asked. Marcus stayed silent.

"Well I hope you've got more than that for the judge," the officer said. "You're going away for a *long* time." He put a big emphasis on the word long; like it was actually going to be a really long time. Even Marcus knew that murder gets you twenty-five to life. Marcus has spent twenty-eight times that already on earth. What would another twenty-five years prove? He sat in silence. Another police car pulled up. The passenger got out and walked over to the driver's side door of the car Marcus was sitting in. "So, what's the deal?" the new officer asked.

"This guy in the back had a sword fight with that guy on the ground over there. It's obvious who won," the driver replied. The new officer stepped back to the rear window and peered in at Marcus, like he was a zoo animal. "You never can pick 'em," he said. He tapped the roof of the police car and started walking away. The officer in the driver's seat put the car into drive and took off. The officer in the passenger seat was still staring at him.

Ben, Lucifer, Azazel and Asmodeus ran back to Ben's' house, as it wasn't far from where they were. Ben unlocked the door and pushed it open. A large hand grabbed him by the throat, with talons digging into the back of his neck. It pulled him into the lounge room and threw him at the wall behind the couch. He bounced off of the wall and fell onto the couch. Baal grabbed Ben's' bow staff and knocked Azazel out with it, while grabbing Lucifer around the neck. He pulled Lucifer into the room and held him up against the wall next to the door. Asmodeus turned around and ran as fast as he could. "Where is Marcus?" Baal asked Lucifer, who was still up against the wall.

"I don't know!" Lucifer shouted back, as best as he could.

"I think you do," Baal said.

Lucifer squirmed under his large hand. "I don't know. He was just taken away by police for killing one of you fuckers!" Lucifer screamed.

"Oh, that wasn't one of us," Baal snarled. "That was a human." Baal threw Lucifer across the room. He turned around and let out a large burst of flame from his mouth in a giant roar.

CHAPTER V

Marcus was sitting in a room with a large mirror at one end, and a door at the other. He sat in one of two chairs at a cold metal table, with his hands cuffed behind his back. He was staring at the table, as if he could read his own thoughts from it. The door behind him opened. Marcus sat absolutely still as Detective Finn walked around him to the chair on the opposite side of the table. He placed a small tape recorder on the table and pressed record. "Please state your name for the record," Detective Finn said. Marcus looked up from his spot on the table, and into the Detective's eyes. He was in a blue grey suit and had a black goatee above a black tie. His hair was short, and his skin was not white, but tanned. He stared back into Marcus' eyes. "Name, please?" he asked.

Marcus sat forward with no expression. "Marcus," he finally said.

"Thank you, Marcus. I'm Detective Matthew Finn. I'm just going to be asking you a few questions. Is that okay?"

"Fine by me," Marcus replied.

"Okay then," Detective Finn started. "Can I please have your last name?"

"Don't have one."

"You don't have one? Everybody has a last name."

"I don't," Marcus said.

"Okay, are you aware of why you're here?" Detective Finn asked.

"I'm going to take a stab at homicide," Marcus smirked. "No pun intended."

"Well now I know that you knew what you were doing. Can I ask why you did it?"

"Nope, I'm afraid not," Marcus said, as he sat back.

"I'm going to need to know," Detective Finn said.

"May I please have a cigarette?" Marcus asked.

Detective Finn looked at him for a long second and nodded his head, as he reached into his jacket pocket and came out with a soft packet of cigarettes. He pulled one out and reached across to put it in Marcus' mouth. Marcus leaned forward to accept the cigarette, as Finn pulled a chrome lighter out of his pants pocket with the other hand, and lit the cigarette for Marcus. He put the lighter back in his pocket as

Marcus drew a long deep breath of smoke. He opened one side of his mouth to let the smoke drift out, while the other side of his mouth firmly held the cigarette. He tensed his shoulders and wrenched his arms apart, breaking the chain on the handcuffs. Detective Finn stood up and stepped back, scraping his chair across the floor. Marcus put one hand to his mouth and closed his thumb and finger on the cigarette to take it out of his mouth. He put both arms on the table with a clink of the handcuffs on the cold steel. The Detective slowly sat back down. "How did you do that? Those are made out of reinforced steel," he asked.

Marcus looked down at the handcuffs and shrugged. The door opened and another man in a suit stepped in. "Everything okay in here?" he asked.

"Fine, thank you," Finn replied. The man looked at Marcus and back at Finn, and left the room.

"Now, you need to clear some things up for me. You have no identification, you have no finger prints, no last name, and the strength of a dozen men. But as far as I'm concerned, you don't exist. And nobody will miss you," Finn said.

"Yes, nobody and I get along well," Marcus replied.

"Don't get smart with me, Marcus. You're in a lot of trouble."

"I don't think so," Marcus replied.

Marcus' blue wings started rising up out of his back. They grew and filled the entire room. Detective Finn dropped his jaw, and looked up in awe at the wings. He looked into Marcus' eyes. "What are you?" he asked.

"Guess," Marcus replied.

Two more Detectives burst into the room. "What the hell is that?" one of them asked.

Finn shook his head, staring up at the wings. "I'm still not sure," he said. "I'm afraid to say it, but they look like wings."

"Wings?" one of the other Detectives said. "Bullshit."

He reached forward to try and touch the blue mist. At the same time, part of Marcus' wings latched onto the Detectives arm. Marcus stood up as his wing let go of the Detective. "Detective Finn, could you please ask these men to leave?" Marcus asked politely.

"Get out of here, you two," Finn said. "I'm fine here."

The two men left the room. Detective Finn looked at Marcus. "An angel, right?" he asked.

"Pretty much. I can't be held here. There is too much at stake," Marcus replied.

"Like what?" Finn asked.

"I can't tell you. You're just gonna have to let me go."

"I'm afraid I can't do that Marcus. Not without clearance."

"You'll get your clearance. Get me Declan from the Paranormal Division of the FBI."'

"There's no Paranormal Division," Finn said.

"Oh, yes there is. Declan is an old friend of mine. Just tell him that you have Marcus in custody, and he'll be here as soon as possible."

"Okay, I'll try and get a hold of him. But I'm going to have to put you in a cell for the time being," Finn said.

"That's fine with me. I can wait," Marcus replied.

Finn went to walk out of the room. He stopped and turned back to Marcus. "Just one more thing. If you're an angel, can't you just disappear and go back to Heaven?"

"Not exactly. Since I have been arrested I am unable to do anything. If an angel is taken into custody by human law enforcement, they're on their own," Marcus said.

"So, how can this Declan guy help?" Finn asked.

"Because he is part of human law enforcement. And besides, we're old friends. He owes me."

"I'll take your word for it," Finn said, as he walked out the door. Marcus picked up the tape recorder.

Finn walked to his office and sat behind his desk, trying to understand exactly what was going on. He felt a little disheartened and also a little fearful, now knowing that angels walked the earth. He picked up the hand piece of the telephone and hesitantly dialed a number from memory. The phone rang in his ear and was answered almost instantly. "Federal Bureau of Investigation, New York Office. How may I direct your call?" the voice on the other end asked.

Finn let out a brief sigh. "Detective Matthew Finn calling from the 13th precinct. I need to speak to a Declan, in some... Paranormal Division? As ludicrous as that sounds."

"One moment, please."

There was a brief moment of hold music, and then the phone began ringing in his ear again. He waited a few moments until it was answered. "Federal Bureau of Investigation. How may I help you?"

Finn sat forward. "Didn't I just do this?" Finn asked.

"I'm sorry sir, you've been transferred to me from the front desk. Is there someone in particular you're after?"

"Yes," Finn answered irately. "Declan, Paranormal Division. Is someone playing a joke here?"

"That depends on the nature of the call. What is it regarding?"

Finn sighed again. "Apparently, an angel named Marcus."

"One moment, please."

Finn waited a moment and was instantly transferred to another phone within FBI Headquarters. "Declan here. What about Marcus?"

Finn sat up straight. "So, you *do* exist. I thought Marcus might have been putting me through the ringer."

"Detective, get to the point, please," Declan barked.

"I have him here. He was arrested for murder."

"Murder?"

"Yep, he struck someone down in the street, with a sword, which magically disappeared."

"I'll be right there."

The phone went silent and clicked off, as a shrill tone echoed from the earpiece. He laid the phone back into its cradle on his desk, and stood up to exit his office. He calmly opened his door and closed it behind him, as he proceeded toward the interrogation room. He opened the door to find Marcus still sitting at the table, with his fingers linked together, and the tape recorder sitting only inches away from his hands. "Okay, we have gotten a hold of Declan. He'll be here very soon. But for now, I have to put you in a cell whilst I meet with him." Finn picked up the tape recorder.

"You might want to listen to that later. Alone," Marcus said. Finn held the tape recorder up to his face and inspected it closely. "Oh, I left it recording." He pressed the stop button as he put it in his pocket. He looked warily at Marcus. "You know," he said, "Angel or not, you're obviously a menace to society. Why shouldn't I let you rot in prison, since you're bound by law enforcement?"

Marcus looked up. "Do you see any demons, in their true form, roaming the streets freely?"

Finn shook his head with intrigue. "You're welcome," Marcus said. Finn uncomfortably shook his head; not sure whether he should be grateful or terrified. He left the room and the two officers that burst in earlier, came in and picked Marcus up to take him to his holding cell. They walked out of the door and into a bright corridor, where many policemen and men in suits were walking around. To Marcus' right were the doors out to the lobby, and to his left were the doors that led further into the precinct, and to the holding cells. The two officers walked Marcus to the left, toward the double doors at the end and pushed through them into a medium sized room with three cells to the left, and desks and more policemen to the right. They put Marcus in the middle cell and closed the door behind him, as he took a moment to survey his current living situation. He was sure Declan could get him out. Then he heard it.

Shunk...

Marcus turned around. The room was deserted; all but one was left in the room. It was Orias. He didn't have his normal look, as he had assumed his human form. He was still enormous, but was now wearing a grey suit that was so big, it must have taken dozens of people to sew together. He was sitting on a desk looking straight at Marcus, the stone in his left hand resting on the blade in his right hand, below his chin.

Shunk...

The rock glided seamlessly across the flat of the blade, sharpening it so finely that it could cut through steel. Marcus knew the blade well. It was sharpened so often, it might even be the sharpest blade in existence, which of course, intrigued Marcus even more. "You know, a blade like that... should really belong to someone who knows how to use it."

Orias smirked. "It bested you, didn't it?"

Now Marcus smiled. "No, that stone in your hand - which I'm assuming belongs to the group of rocks inside your head - may have got the better of me, but your knife has never touched my skin. As I said, be better off with someone who *knows* how to use it."

Orias stood up. "Go on," Marcus beckoned, "throw it at me. I dare you."

Orias slowly walked over to the bars and stood directly in front of the door. Marcus felt a strange reminiscent memory pass through his head, from a similar situation he was in many years earlier. He remembered how he got out of that one, and figured the same idea wouldn't work, as at that time, his captors weren't human. This time, they were. Orias was only visiting. Easier to get someone in prison.

Marcus thought for a second longer. "You know, I still owe you for that lucky shot you got with your little stone." Marcus reached through the bars and grabbed Orias' tie. He used all his strength to pull the tie through the bars, hurtling Orias' head straight for them. It collided with a mighty *clang*, which dazed Orias a little. Marcus pushed him back a little and yanked on the tie again, and again, and again, as Orias kept colliding with the iron bars.

Meanwhile, in another room, Declan had arrived. "You have to let him go!" Declan said. Declan and Detective Finn were sitting in Finn's office. Declan was a tall man, in an expensive blue suit with a matching tie. He sat with his hands together and up to his chin, with his long index fingers pointing at his lips.

"I can't just let him walk out of here, sir," Finn replied. "He's been arrested for manslaughter, with two officers as witnesses."

"If I know Marcus, and believe me, I do, if he's started killing things, then there's a reason for it. And, I think I know what that reason is," Declan replied.

"What is it? I need to know these things."

"You don't need to know anything. I can't have it in a New York Police file that an angel was arrested for murder. Albeit, a human was involved. I can't allow such a report to be filed. You're going to have to release him to me. You, of all people should know that a case like this won't end pretty. There will be a long trial, with countless numbers of psychiatrists, and an ending that will have you busted down the ranks along with years of therapy. I know you don't want that."

Detective Finn sat for a long moment. His eyes shifted from side to side, like he was weighing up his options. "Suppose I let him go. What do I put in my report?" he asked Declan.

"You report that the suspect was released to the FBI for further investigations involving other crimes, and nobody will touch you. Shred every document you have on him, please," Declan replied.

Finn breathed out. He looked deflated, like all the air had just been let out of him. "Okay, he's all yours."

Declan stood up and walked out of the room and into a brightly lit corridor towards the double doors, with big windows covering the top half. He burst through them and saw the three cells on his left. In the middle one, he saw

Marcus yanking on the tie of the largest man Declan had ever seen. The man's head was bouncing off the bars, again and again. Declan almost put a stop to it, when he realised who it was. "Shit!" he screeched. "It's Orias!"

"No shit!" Marcus said, as he kept pulling on the tie, speaking with every collision. "Hit! Me! With! That! Rock! Again! I'll..."

"Okay, enough. Let's kill him already!"
Orias awakened from his concussed stupor and instantly disappeared in a cloud of black smoke. "Well, be grateful no one else saw that. You'd be in a lot more trouble."

"You got me off, right?"

"I've pulled some strings and can only get you twenty-five years," Declan said.

"You mean twenty-five years working for you, you dirty bastard!" Marcus replied.

"Okay, yes you got me. You're off the hook. But, I need details. For starters, why are you killing people? The only reason I can think of is that you killed a demon. But then, they would turn into a muddy pulp and any officers that saw it would have figured it for a hallucination. What's going on Marcus?"

Marcus pulled a cigarette out of his jacket pocket and lighter out of his pants pocket. He lit the cigarette and breathed out a long breath of smoke. "I know where it is," he said calmly.

"Well then, you have to stop wasting people in the public eye. You know I can't help you every time! So, enlighten me. Where is it?"

Marcus pulled a long drag of his cigarette and exhaled the toxic fumes. "Guarding the entrance to paradise," he said.

Detective Finn burst through the double doors and stared at Marcus. "So, you had cigarettes this whole time? Didn't anybody take them off you?" he asked. "Why did you have to have one of mine?"

"First things first. My hands were bound behind my back, and second, you had me in that room for a long time. From what I recall, you didn't exactly empty my pockets."

"Well if we ever cross paths again, I assure you that's the first thing I'll do."

Finn opened the cell. The door rattled open with a loud clang as he noticed the bars were bent inwards. Quite drastically inwards, as if something large had been smashed into them. Marcus walked over to Declan. "Good day, Detective. You did a good job, for what it's worth," Marcus said.

"Yeah, yeah. What the hell happened here?"

Marcus shrugged, and looked up at the surveillance camera in the corner. "Maybe check that out, too."

"Alright, get out of here," Finn muttered and waved a hand at them. Marcus and Declan walked through the double doors and down a long corridor towards the exit. They were side by side, and walking fast with a new-found sense of hope. Declan opened the doors and Marcus felt the fresh air hit his nose. He took a deep breath in. "Ahh, the smell of freedom," he said.

Declan raised his eyebrows and stared at Marcus. "You've been in there maybe four hours. How can you possibly be gratified by the sense of freedom? Come on, we're wasting valuable time," Declan said.

They turned left and walked quickly. "So, tell me everything that's happened so far," Declan said. "I want details. No sugar coating."

Marcus took a drag of his cigarette and let the smoke drift out his nose. "Okay," he started. "It all started when some demons came looking for the sword. They thought I already had it, then my friend Ben and I got a visit from Eran, the Throne."

"Who is Ben?" Declan asked.

"He is a human, but he has been given wings now after we went to Hell."

"You took a human to Hell?" Declan snapped.

"I had to! Marcus shouted back. "Eran said I had to. Shut up and listen, would you?"

Declan rolled his eyes. "Okay, continue," he sighed.

"So anyway, we got a visit from Eran, and Ben figured out that my sword was the very same one guarding the entrance to Eden. He's a smart kid. I realised that finding Eden was just about the same as finding peace on Earth, but then Eran gave me the idea of using somebody who has been there before."

"Please tell me you didn't." Declan turned away and put his hands on his head.

"I did. It was the only way," Marcus replied.

"You dragged your brother into this? How do we even know that Lucifer will be trustworthy? And this Ben fellow, you think he might be involved with the Revelation?" Declan glared at Marcus.

"Lucifer is trustworthy in this matter. He's my brother, and he would never deceive me. And as for Ben, I don't think he has the power within him to be the human angel. Besides, his wings are white, not gold," Marcus said.

"Okay," Declan gave in, "whatever you say Marcus. Please, keep going."

"So, we got Lucifer involved, and you can't involve him without involving the idiot twins. Now, we have Azazel and Asmodeus hovering around us."

"I wouldn't trust them as far as I could throw them." Declan thought for a second. "No wait, scratch that. I would throw them pretty far given the opportunity, so I wouldn't trust them if my life depended on it."

"You wouldn't trust *anything* if your life depended on it. So, we killed a few demons, we crossed Baal, Orias and Eligos in the Chislehurst caves, and then we went to see Samael for some answers. Then, I got arrested, and you know the rest."

Declan looked at the ground as he walked. There were questions in his eyes. "What is it?" Marcus asked him.

"First thing's first. How many demons have you come across since leaving Hell?"

Marcus looked up to his right, trying hard to recall the details, as if looking up to that side of his brain would help him.
"Two since leaving Hell, and Baal. Then Orias and Eligos, and Orias again."

"So, this is pretty big then. You have somebody among you that is giving Beelzebub details of what you're doing," Declan said.

"But, nobody has been alone long enough to contact anybody," Marcus said.

Declan rolled his eyes. "You should know better than anyone that you don't need to be alone to contact anyone on the down low. For starters, I wouldn't be trusting the idiot twins. I'd send them to Purgatory right now if I were you. It's the same as possession. They just have to be present and be collecting all the data, and they send it off to a main processor. Like computers," Declan said.

"I have no idea how computers work, so you'll have to spare me the metaphors. But, I think I understand what you're saying. Funnily enough, I think I'm actually warming up to Azazel. He seems to be sincerely happy to be working with us. Asmodeus, I'm not sure about." Marcus took another puff of his cigarette.

They continued walking down the familiar street towards the front door of Marcus' apartment. Marcus used his key in the door and they walked towards the elevator. Marcus pushed the number 3 on the elevator wall, and the doors closed.

"You know, this is bigger than you could ever imagine. They've even stooped to possessions to get you. And, they nearly had you out of the picture with this one. You know how easily they could have gotten you in prison? If you hadn't overpowered Orias. I'm still not sure how you did that with his gigantism, but anyway, you'd be done for," Declan said.

"I know," Marcus said, "thank you."

The elevator made a small 'ping' noise as they reached the third floor. Marcus walked out of the elevator, followed by Declan. He walked down the hallway to his apartment door, and put a finger up in the air as a 'wait' gesture to Declan. He pulled his sword out from under his jacket and thrust it through his front door. He pulled his key out and unlocked the door, and swung it open. There was a small muddy cement like puddle just inside the hallway entrance. Declan looked down at the puddle. "I'm getting sick of killing these fucking things!" Marcus shouted.

"How did you know there was a demon there?" he asked.

Marcus put his sword back up under his jacket. "Why wouldn't there be?" Marcus said, gesturing to the crosses on the hallway walls and ceiling. Declan looked down at the rug on the floor and moved over to it. He threw a corner of it back to reveal a cross painted on the floor. "A holy seal. Good work. But demons can transport too, you know?"

Marcus smiled as he kicked the rug back into shape and walked out of the hallway into his lounge room. "You think I would take the bare minimum of risks? The alarm is wired up to the sprinkler system," he said.

"Let me guess. You've blessed the water that runs to the sprinklers."

"It's the only way they'll learn," Marcus said.

Declan looked around the apartment and fixed his gaze on the broken window. "Trouble?" he asked.

"A few days ago. I had a visit from the three," Marcus replied.

"The three? He actually walked the earth? No doubt he wanted the sword," Declan asked.

"He thought I already had it. Shows how far behind they are."

"Marcus! He walked the earth in three! You know the passage, he will walk the earth, but he will walk in three. Beelzebub came to earth. Not only that, he came to your front door. This is big!"

"I know!"

"Well, stop treating it like another stroll in the park! Where are you meeting the others?" Declan asked.

"At Ben's place. It's not too far from here," Marcus replied.

He fiddled with the pendant around his neck. "I'd better leave this here for safe keeping," he said.

"You sure it's safe here?" Declan asked.

Marcus looked at the sprinkler system. "Yeah, I'm sure."

"Why do you want to leave that here anyway?" Declan asked.

"Because there was a demon here. If there was one here, then sure enough, there was one at Ben's house. I don't want to risk losing anything that I need."

Marcus unlatched the chain necklace from behind his neck and left it on the coffee table. "Come on, let's go," he said. They walked back out through the entrance hallway and out the front door.

* * *

Baal smacked Lucifer in the face with Ben's staff. They were all tied to a load bearing pillar in between the lounge room and the kitchen. "It's no good anyway. You'll never get your hands on the sword," Lucifer said. Baal looked at him with his large, red eyes. He smacked him across the face with the staff again. "I'll be the judge of that!" Baal roared. "You're two men down. You don't have a fighting chance."

Lucifer gave off a small smile. "What are you grinning at?" Baal asked.

"We have Declan. You really think Marcus will stay locked up for long?" he asked.

"I'm taking all necessary actions to make sure he comes right here. In fact, I'm expecting the two of them very shortly."

Baal stepped over to Ben. "So, you're the prodigy. Marcus' apprentice," he said.

"Give me my staff back, and I'll show you," Ben said.

Baal huffed and swatted Ben with his own staff. Baal looked up and smirked. "They're here," he said. He disappeared.

The front door opened and Marcus and Declan silently walked in. Marcus had his sword in his hand. They both saw Ben, Lucifer and Azazel tied to the pillar in the centre of the room. "Get out of here!" Lucifer shouted. "It's a trap. Baal is here!"

Marcus turned around and was grabbed by the throat. Baal picked him up off the ground and hoisted him into the air. "You're late." Baal said.

"And you're ugly," Marcus struggled to say. "But I can change."

Baal threw Marcus at the pillar. The pillar bent and the roof sagged above Ben, Lucifer and Azazel. Baal knocked Declan over and picked Marcus up. He tied him up with the other three to the pillar, but standing with him, hands tied around the pillar in front of him. Baal walked over to Declan on the floor, and sat on him. "So, tell me Marcus," Baal said, "where is it?"

"Where is what?" Marcus asked.

"The last artefact, of course," Baal replied. "You know exactly what I'm talking about. I have the staff, and after I kill you, I'll have those trinkets you wear. There's just one last thing after that. Need all of them to get the sword."

Lucifer tried to sit up. "There are no more artifacts you ugly, stinking, rotting carcass!" he shouted.

"Of course, there are. Just ask Marcus," Baal said.

Lucifer looked at Marcus. "There are other artifacts?" he asked.

"Yes, there is another artifact."

"You piece of shit. I told you everything I know, and you're hiding things from me? Why didn't you tell me? I trusted you!" Lucifer shouted. "We're brothers, for fuck's sake!"

"Will you shut up?" Marcus shouted back. "You're not helping the situation."

Baal switched his gaze between the two brothers shouting back and forth at each other. Marcus was standing up at the pillar, with his hands tied around its now broken centre, while the other three were sitting at the base of it, with their arms tied around it behind their backs. Baal sat up and off of Declan, and held a sword to his throat. "Tell me where it is!" he shouted. Declan awoke from his daze.

"Don't tell him Marcus!" he yelled.

"Don't worry, I won't," Marcus replied.

Baal looked down at Declan and slit his throat. Declan burst into the same cement-like liquid as the demons when they were killed. Marcus, Lucifer, Ben and Azazel all looked in horror. "You know what, Lucifer? You *are* helping. Keep screaming" Marcus said.

He yanked his hands towards the pillar, breaking it completely in half. The roof sagged even more as Marcus ripped his hands apart, breaking the supernatural rope binding them together. He launched himself at Baal and landed on top of him. He grabbed him around the neck from behind, and forced him down onto the ground. Lucifer awkwardly tried to stand up against the pillar and forced his arms out of the gap Marcus left. He worked his arms down below his legs and stepped over the bindings, so that his arms were now in front of him. He reached behind Ben and set him free. Ben stood up and helped Lucifer untie himself and Azazel. They all stood up and looked at Marcus who had a strong hold of Baal's thick neck. He was forcing Baal's face to the ground and looking up at Ben, Lucifer and Azazel. "Where's Asmodeus?" he asked.

"He escaped," Lucifer said. "He saw Baal and ran for it."

Ben looked down at the second muddy puddle on his floor. "Why did he die, the same way as the demons?" he asked.

"Because he's gone to Purgatory. Like I told you before, about when angels are killed by demons," Lucifer replied.

"Oh, that can't be good," he said.

Marcus lifted Baal's face off of the floor. "You gonna play nice?" he asked him. Baal stayed silent. "Who's telling you our movements?" Marcus asked.

A smile formed on Baal's big, demonic face. "If you haven't figured that out yet, then you won't survive," he laughed.

"That's it, I've heard enough," Marcus said.

He pulled his sword out from under his jacket and spun it around, holding it in both hands below the knuckles. He stabbed Baal in the back of the head. Baal roared in pain. Marcus pulled his sword out and plunged it straight back into the open wound again, and again, and again. The world around the two of them changed. The ground was like wet cement. There were decaying bodies lying around them. Baal kicked and squirmed under Marcus, gasping and looking up at the other three with pain in his eyes. Marcus thrust the sword into his head one last time, and moved his arms away from him, like he was pushing on a lever. The sword split the back of Baal's head wide open. Baal burst into flames and disintegrated. Marcus jumped up quickly and away from the flames. He was breathing heavily. He was back in Ben's house, standing next to Ben and watching as the flames died away.

"What the hell was *that*?" Ben asked.

Lucifer looked in awe at the ashes on the floor, and then up at Marcus. "You killed him," he said. "I mean, you actually killed him. How did you do that?"

Marcus let out a deep breath and looked at Lucifer. "Oh, come on, you know how it works. If you die in Purgatory, there's no coming back," Marcus said.

Lucifer kept looking between the ashes and Marcus. "But we're not in Purgatory," Lucifer said. "You killed him right over there on the floor."

Lucifer pointed to the ashes as he said it. Marcus' eyes followed to where his finger was pointing. "Okay, that's a little strange. I transported the two of us to Purgatory. How the hell did you all see it?"

"I don't know," Ben said. "But that was pretty spectacular."

Marcus wiped his sword on the floor and put it back up under his jacket. "Hey!" Ben yelled. "These aren't exactly cheap carpets, you know!"

Marcus looked at Ben, and then at the puddles and ashes on the carpet. "Yeah, it's not exactly clean either," Marcus said. Ben nodded.

"Good point," he said. "So, where to now?"

"To St. Andrews," Marcus said. "We need somewhere safe to talk."

Ben walked over to the couch and picked up his bow staff. Marcus grabbed him on the shoulder and they were instantly standing in the same church as when they were talking to Eran. Ben slung his bow staff over his shoulder. Lucifer and Azazel came walking in from the entrance. Azazel was very hesitant about crossing the threshold. "It's okay, you're working with us. You're welcome in here." Azazel stepped forward with a sigh of relief and joined the others. "Tell me about the last artifact," Lucifer said.

Marcus sighed. "It's the pendant. Baal was talking about the pendant."

"It's the Amulet of the Shadows. We know that. Why is it so special to us now, though?"

Marcus looked up at Lucifer. "Because it's part of the sword," he said.

Lucifer looked at him in shock. "As in, part of *your* sword?"

"Yes, my sword. When I made it, a piece chipped off. I was devastated, until God put it on a necklace and gave it to me. Of course, with my sword in my hand and the pendant around my neck, it was still very powerful. Arus used my sword in the last war, after you were cast out. Unfortunately, the sword was too powerful and didn't exactly do what Arus wanted it to. It killed Nikolas."

Lucifer looked at Marcus a little harder. "Nikolas is dead?" he asked.

"Yes, killed by my sword. Angel blood was spilled and it was taken away from me. The Revelation says that the sword will spill human blood by the hand of evil, and that the two pieces will then merge, making the sword complete.

"Well that's good, isn't it?" Ben asked.

"No," Marcus said. "It means that the sword will fall into the wrong hands, and then become complete. After that, the sword will then smite its possessor. I don't know if that will be me, or someone else. And to be honest, I'm not really looking forward to finding that out."

Lucifer looked at the ground, and then back up at Marcus. "Okay, so we need the staff, the pendant, and Arus' belt and cuffs?"

"Yes," Marcus said. "I need to be wearing them when I get the sword, and the staff is the way to Eden."

Ben looked at Marcus' neck and saw that the pendant was missing. "Where is the pendant?" he asked.

"It's safe," Marcus said. "Let's go and get it."

CHAPTER VI

The elevator made the same 'ping' noise as they reached the third floor of Marcus' apartment. Marcus walked down the corridor to his front door, while the other three followed. He pulled his keys out and stopped for a second. He noticed his door was open. He put the keys away and pulled his sword out from under his jacket. He kicked the door open and saw Asmodeus standing in the hallway entrance, trapped between the door and the crosses. "A holy seal," he said. "Very clever. A little help please?" Marcus walked straight past him and into the lounge room. The others watched from the door. He walked to the coffee table and picked up the pendant. He slowly put it around his neck, looking at Asmodeus. "What are you doing here?" Marcus asked.

"I thought you'd come here after they released you," Asmodeus replied.

"Ahh, but how did you know I would be released? You know the rules - every angel for himself on Earth," Marcus said.

"Yes but," Asmodeus tried to speak.

"Oh, cut the crap!" Marcus yelled. "I know it was you!"

Marcus raised his sword. Asmodeus disappeared. "I'm gonna kill him!" Marcus said. Azazel looked through the doorway. "Will I get in there?" he asked.

Marcus looked at him. "You can transport past the seal. Don't worry, the sprinklers aren't on," he said.

"Sprinklers?" Ben asked.

"Holy water," Marcus said. "If they get past the seal, they get wet."

Ben looked up at the sprinkler system on the ceiling. "You mean holy water and crosses actually work?" Ben asked.

"To a degree," Lucifer said. "But for demons and fallen angels. You can bet on it that Baal could have gotten past it. The holy water certainly would be painful to him, though."

They all walked through the hallway and into the room, except for Azazel, who transported past the crosses. He reappeared in the lounge room. Ben took his bow staff off his shoulder and placed it against the wall. Marcus walked over to the bookshelf and pushed it. It spun around in the wall, revealing a second bookcase from the opposite side. The bookshelf was filled with old leather-bound books, all handwritten journals of Marcus'. Ben watched as he did it, and walked over to inspect the books. Marcus perused through, looking for one in particular.

"American Civil War, American Revolution..." Ben read aloud, as he looked through the shelf. His eyes settled on a book on the second shelf down. "The Golden Age of Piracy?" Ben went to pull the book down off the shelf as Marcus slapped his hand. "Did I say you could read them?"

"What are they?" Ben asked.

"They're my writings. My whole life on earth is here. Except for one thing." The books were all in alphabetical order, and the entire shelf was full, except for one gap between 'C' and 'E'. Ben found the gap. "Is that what's supposed to be here? Guessing it starts with D?"

Marcus let out an uncomfortable sigh. Pain filled his eyes as he remembered the events of the missing book. "Downfall?" Lucifer asked. Marcus stayed silent, but his discomfort grew as he looked away. "Good lord, you actually have a detailed record of it? No one knows what happened to you there, but whatever it was, it certainly did something to you. Something bad. I remember seeing the change in you afterwards. I'd give anything to read that journal."

"What's Downfall?" Ben asked.

"None of your damn business," Marcus said. "Any of you." Everyone stared in an awkward silence. Marcus walked over to the window and looked out, as he leaned on the window sill with his arm up in front of his face. He rested his forehead on his bicep as he stared out at the street. There was a small cabinet with a flat screen television sitting on top of it, just to

Marcus' left. The cabinet itself was full of television accessories, a DVD player, and a PlayStation, among other things. Marcus looked towards it, as memories flooded back into his head. His rage built as he tried to subdue the images he could see, of things that happened so long ago he'd almost forgotten. But, the pain was still there. His anger grew as he began to breathe heavily, and he reached down grabbing hold of the cabinet and flinging it almost across the room with great strength. It didn't hit anyone, luckily, but it certainly made quite a mess. Marcus stood and looked at the cabinet and television in pieces, as he calmed himself. He glared at Lucifer. "You mention that place again, I will fucking end you," he said through his teeth. Lucifer gulped and made a zipping gesture on his mouth to signify compliant silence.

Marcus walked back over to the bookshelf and pulled out an old notebook with nothing written on the spine. It was brown and leather bound, with a latch that clipped around the front to keep it closed. He unlatched it and opened it, and flicked through the pages as he walked over to the couch. He placed the book on the table as Lucifer sat next to him. "Okay," Marcus said, pointing to the open page, "this is the Persian Gulf." He put his finger on the map on the page. It was drawn with ink. Marcus moved his finger to a spot on the page that looked like an island in a body of water. "This is supposedly where Eden is supposed to be," he said. "Where the four rivers meet."

Ben hovered over the coffee table and looked at the page. "You mean, you've already tried to find Eden?" he asked.

Marcus and Lucifer looked up at him. "Hey, if I'd have known my sword was there, I would have tried a little harder," he replied. He moved his finger to the side of the Gulf on the page and tapped on some writing that said KUWAIT CITY. "We can get a boat there, avoid the war zone, and plunge straight out into the Gulf," he said. Marcus moved his hand away from the book so that Lucifer could get a closer look. Lucifer picked up the book and inspected the page closely. He lowered the book and looked at Marcus. "You know, this might actually be possible," he said.

"Of course, it is," Marcus said. "I wouldn't have suggested it otherwise." Ben stepped over to Marcus' computer and turned it on. Marcus looked at him as he moved. Once the computer was finished booting up, it opened up into Microsoft Windows, with a small tune coming from the speakers. Ben opened the internet browser and found himself at the Google website. "Okay, well let's go to Kuwait," Lucifer said as he put the book down on the table. He left the page open.

"Hold on a second," Marcus said. "We need to source a boat, we need to make sure we've got everything we need, and make sure we're not going to run into anyone that we don't want to." Marcus pointed to the page on the book again. He put his finger just below the writing on the map.

"There's a place to the south of Kuwait called Fahaheel Waterfront, in Al Kout. There's a marina there and they hold an annual boat show around this time of year. Lots of boat sales. We can easily spend big bucks and buy a boat without anyone thinking otherwise," he said.

"A boat show, hey?" Lucifer asked. "How big is it?"

"It's huge," Marcus said. "The Kuwait International Boat Show. It's usually around the start of May, which is now. We need something big enough for the four of us, and something that can handle the waters in the Gulf. Lucifer, I'll need you to shop around the boat show and pick something suitable. Ben, we're going to need somewhere to stay. A hotel, a tourist residence, anything you can find."

"I'm already on it," Ben replied.

Marcus looked at Lucifer. "Doing this by the book." Lucifer nodded. "You know," he said as he looked at his little brother, "I like *this* you. *This* you is much better than the drunk you've been lately. *This* you has purpose and motivation. Whatever happened in Downfall, it happened, it's in the past. It doesn't define you."

Marcus lowered his head in shame. "If you knew, you'd be singing a different tune."

"So, enlighten me. You don't have to carry that burden alone. You have me, and Azazel considers you a friend now." Lucifer looked at Ben. "And this kid? This kid would walk through fire for you."

Marcus looked up. "He already has," Marcus said.

"He is a true friend. You owe it to him, especially now that he's involved in the biggest part of your story. You owe it to all of us, to be the best you that you can be. This whole thing is for you. You realise that, yes? We're all here, for you. Don't dismiss that. Whatever demons plague your past, you still have us."

They put their foreheads together in a brotherly embrace. "I know."

Ben had the web browser on a page with Hilton Kuwait Resort written at the top. "This looks perfect," he said over his shoulder. "It's in Fahaheel, and is walking distance to the waterfront."

"Perfect, I've been there before," Marcus said. "Book it for tonight."

"The Hilton?" Lucifer asked. "Isn't that going to be expensive?"

"I'll handle the money," Marcus replied. "I have enough to cover my expenses."

"How could you possibly have enough to buy a brand new boat, and rent four rooms at the Hilton hotel in Kuwait?" Ben asked.

"Hey, I've been on Earth for seven hundred years," Marcus said. "I think I've had enough time to build myself a small fortune. Book it."

"Okay," Ben said. He clicked on a small button on the page to book the rooms.

"Make it two rooms," Marcus said. "Two singles in each. Ben, you and I can share a room, and you two will have to do the same." He walked into his kitchen and opened the third draw down. He pulled out a credit card and a British passport and threw the credit card to Ben. "Here, use this," he said. Ben caught the credit card and began punching in the numbers. Marcus walked over to Lucifer and put the passport in his hand. "That's your credit card, and this is your passport." Lucifer opened up the passport and saw a photo that looked almost just like him. The name next to the photo said Davis, Luke. Below that was a date of birth. Lucifer was impressed. "Alright, I'm a human. How did you get this?" Lucifer asked.

"I have my ways," Marcus replied. "That's for identification if you need to show any."

"I have a question," Azazel said.

"What is it?" Marcus asked.

"What if we *are* followed? I mean, I remember that sound we heard in the cave. That was Orias. He's not one to be trifled with. Nasty piece of work. I'm surprised you made it out alive, and very impressed," he said. Marcus nodded with a newfound respect for Azazel. "We'll deal with that when and if it happens," Marcus said.

"Okay," Azazel said.

"Hotel is booked," Ben said over his shoulder, as he handed the card back to Marcus, who then handed it to Lucifer.

"How much was it?" Marcus asked.

"Twelve hundred and eighteen dollars, and ninety cents," Ben replied.

"Good. We're set. I'll take Ben with me, and we'll meet you two at the hotel. Ben, get the staff." Ben walked over to his staff and threw it over his shoulder with the strap. Marcus walked to the table and closed the notebook and latched it. He slid it in his inner pocket in his jacket. "Okay, see you there," Lucifer said. Marcus grabbed Ben on the shoulder and they disappeared. Lucifer and Azazel took the hint and transported out of Marcus' apartment. The room was quiet and still. Asmodeus reappeared in the doorway. A wicked smile smoothed over his angry boyish face. "Perfect," he said, as if the others were still in the room. "I'll see you there."

They found themselves in a hotel room with a red and white theme. There were crisp white bed sheets with a red throw rug, lying across both beds. "Wow, I can't believe that actually worked," Marcus said.

"Where are we?" Ben asked.

"We're in one of the rooms at the Hilton in Kuwait," Marcus replied. Ben looked around the room, and then at Marcus. "You've been here before, haven't you?" he asked.

"Yep, and if I'm not mistaken, this is room 5." He walked to the door, opened it quietly, and looked out into the hallway. It was empty. He stepped out of the room and Ben followed him into the hallway. Marcus tapped the number on the door. "See? I told you. Room 5," he said. They walked down the hallway and came out into a large lobby. Ben walked up to the counter to speak to the desk clerk. She was olive skinned with dark black hair. Ben put on his charming smile. "I have a reservation for Ben Waters," he said. The clerk tapped on the keyboard in front of her. "For Ben Waters," she said. "Two rooms with two single beds in each. May I please see some identification?" She had a terrific accent, Ben thought. And a smile to match. She was very fluent in speaking English. He supposed she had to be, to work at the Hilton.

"No problems," he said, as he reached into his pocket and pulled out his wallet. He opened it up and flipped open a little window. He pulled his New York drivers licence out from behind it, and handed it to the woman. She inspected it and looked at him. He smiled. She handed his license back to him. "Thank you, Ben," she said. "Rooms five and six," she said, as she handed him two small envelopes with rectangular wallet sized cards in them. "Those are your key cards for your rooms. May I please have a credit card to attach to the rooms?" she asked.

"Why do you need that?" Ben asked.

"For the mini bar, and any other of our services you may use."

"Okay, I guess," Ben said. He pulled out his credit card and handed it to her. He looked back at Marcus with a nod and a smile. Marcus nodded back. He turned back to the woman. She handed his credit card back to him. "Enjoy your stay, Mr. Waters," she said with a smile.

"Thank you," Ben said.

They walked back down the hall to room 5. Ben put the card in the slot and the door clicked. Ben turned the handle and they both walked back into the room. Ben took his bow staff off his shoulder and put it down beside the bed closest to the door, and then sat down on the bed. There was a large window at the end of the room, looking out over the pool. Marcus walked over to the window and looked out to the pool area. It was nearing dusk. He sat on the bed closest to the window and threw himself backwards onto the bed, with his arm over his face. He closed his eyes.

Azazel and Lucifer walked around the marina for a few hours, surveying the exhibition spaces. There were boats at the docks as far as the eye could see. They visited many docks and looked at various boats, asking specific questions to all vendors, like "how much?" and, "can we have the display model today?", but, they all said no. After a while, they found a vendor that looked rather desperate. He had a few boats behind him, and was eyeing off every potential onlooker as they walked past. Lucifer knew the look. The vendor stood up straight and put on his charming smile, and walked over. "Good afternoon to you sir! Would you like to take a look at some of the finest vessels here today?"

Lucifer raised an eyebrow and tried to look as business-like as possible. He couldn't quite place his accent, but didn't seem too bothered in finding out where he was from. "Looking for something to use today. Anything in your arsenal up for grabs?" The man looked skeptically at Lucifer. "Oh, these are just for display today. I can have one shipped to you in six weeks," he said.

"Thank you for your time," Lucifer said, as he turned to walk away. The man opened his eyes in desperation. "Wait! Wait, sir," he bumbled. "If you're serious, and your credit checks out, I'm sure I can manage to hand over one of these fine beauties tomorrow." Lucifer turned back to the man with a slightly perturbed look. "Tomorrow? By tomorrow, you do mean right now, correct?" Lucifer pulled out the credit card with his temporary pseudonym, and handed it over to the man.

"I don't think you'll need to do a credit check, I'm fairly sure that will suffice." The vendor took the card and inspected it. It was platinum, with the name Luke Davis extruded in silver letters at the bottom. He seemed impressed by Lucifer. "Surely, there's a daily limit on this. These boats aren't cheap."

Lucifer rolled his eyes. "You're losing me here, boss. Just do the swipe thingy, come on!"

The vendor stared blankly at Lucifer. "Swipey, swipey! That one there." Lucifer pointed to a boat behind the man. "That one. Plenty of space below deck?"

The man nodded. "The Four Winns Vista? Certainly. A few beds, kitchenette and dining, plus bathroom."

"I'll take it."

The vendor nodded, and sat down at his temporary exhibition desk on the dock to write up the paperwork. Lucifer walked up to the back of the boat with Azazel and looked around on the deck. There was a table with bench seats surrounding it on the deck - almost like a diner booth - and beyond that was the captain's chair and wheel, with a seat opposite, and between them, a door that led below. Lucifer turned around to the vendor. "Mind if we take a look?" he asked.

"Of course, it'll be yours by the time you've stepped back on the dock." Lucifer nodded as he and Azazel stepped on board. He walked around to the bow to inspect it, and then back to the driver's seat as he opened the door to the cabin below. There was a bed at the front end, and another tucked down to the right, and two more small beds snuck into places you could barely fit, a kitchenette to his left and a small table in front of him on the right. Next to the table was a small door which was obviously the washroom facilities. He let out a snorted laugh. "Don't shit where you eat, they say." Azazel cracked a slight grin. "It'll do, wouldn't you agree?"

Azazel nodded. "I'm just happy to be along for the ride." Lucifer looked at him with a smirk. He realised that he and

Azazel had similar thinking. "You think we're going to get back in, don't you?" he asked, as he inspected the cabin more, before moving back up to the deck.

"Do you think there's a chance?" Azazel asked.

Lucifer sighed. "I wouldn't bet on it. Although, if the Revelation is true, then a great alliance will be formed. That sentiment alone, has my mind racing. Maybe, in assisting the side of good, we can be redeemed? But, bygones are bygones. And, ours aren't exactly the prettiest."

"Well, I wouldn't be against it, is all I'm saying," Azazel said. "And Marcus, I'm starting to see what everyone says about him. After seeing him take down Baal, twice... let's just say, I'm not planning on messing with him anytime soon."

Lucifer laughed. "I told him we'd all get to see it soon enough. He grows on you, doesn't he?" Azazel smiled. They stepped off the boat and onto the deck, where the vendor handed them the keys. They shook hands and Lucifer and Azazel jumped on board and started the boat. They edged out into marina and worked their way around to the Fahaheel Waterfront, where a large ornamental pool lay just past the docks. Lucifer reversed the boat in and shut it down, as they walked down into the cabin, closed the door behind them and transported away.

There was a knock at the door. Marcus opened one eye and looked out from underneath his arm at Ben. Ben stared back.

Marcus sat up quickly, and put his hand behind his back and up under his jacket. "Open it," he said.

"Me?" Ben asked. "Why me?"

"It's your room," Marcus replied.

Ben stood up and walked to the door. He gripped the handle and turned it slowly, and opened the door an inch. Marcus stood up behind him. Ben peered out through the crack and sighed. He pulled the door open. "It's okay, it's just Lucifer and Azazel," he said. Marcus relaxed. He took his empty hand out from under his jacket. Lucifer and Azazel walked in. "Well, this looks nice," Lucifer said. "Where's our room?"

"Across the hall," Marcus said. "Room 6."

Ben handed Lucifer one of the envelopes with the key card for room 6 in it. "We have a boat," Lucifer said. "A nice big one."

"Great!" Marcus said. "We'll be ready to set sail in the morning?"

"For certain," Lucifer said. "So, what do we do now?"

"Let me guess," Ben said, looking at Marcus. "Where's the bar?"

Marcus looked up at Ben with a very serious look in his eyes. "No, I say we get some rest," Marcus replied. He sat back down on the bed and moved up so that his head would reach the pillow. He lay back down and put his arm back over his face, and fell asleep. Ben and Lucifer looked at each other in a bit of shock. Lucifer nodded. "I think he's right," he said. "We've got a big day tomorrow, and according to the Revelation, there's gonna be a lot more big days to follow."

"I'm gonna have to read this thing one day," Ben said.

"Don't worry, I'll take you to read it myself."

Ben smiled. "So, we're calling it a night?"

"I guess so," Lucifer replied. "We'll set sail first thing tomorrow morning."

Lucifer and Azazel walked out of room 5 and across the hall into their own room. Ben sat back down on his bed and rotated his body to lie down. He put his head on the pillow and looked up at the ceiling. He glanced over at Marcus and then closed his eyes. He fell asleep.

When Ben woke up, he looked over to Marcus' bed and noticed that it was empty. It was dark outside, and the luminous numbers on the clock in between the two beds were showing 2:03. Ben looked around the room and got out of bed. He walked over to the door and opened it up to look out into the hallway. It was empty. He stepped back inside and grabbed the envelope with the key card in it, and slid it into his jacket breast pocket. He walked out of the room, closed the door and walked down the hallway and out past the lobby, and towards the exit doors opposite the desk. He noticed an entrance to the hotel bar to his right, and figured that should be his first port of call. As he walked through the doors, he saw tables all lined up on a forty-five-degree angle to the room. There was a single bartender, and a small figure that Ben recognised instantly at the bar. Marcus had half a glass of amber liquid sitting in front of him. He looked over at Ben and nodded. Ben walked over to him. "I thought you wanted to get some rest," Ben said.

Marcus pointed up at the bottle of Johnnie Walker Blue on the top shelf in an open blue cardboard collector's box. "How can I say no to this?" Marcus asked.

He took a long sip on his drink. He held his glass up as a motion that Ben knew very well. It said *Do you want one?* Ben nodded and sat at the stool next to him. "Another one for my friend here, boss," Marcus said. The bartender reached up to the top shelf and pulled the box down. He removed the blue labeled bottle and poured another glass for Ben, and then left the empty box on the bar and placed the bottle on the bar in between the two of them. He placed Ben's' drink in front of him. "Thank you," Ben said. They both picked up their glasses and took a sip in unison, then took a deep breath after the sip. Ben sat his glass back on the bar. "Like liquid silk," he said.

"I'll drink to that," Marcus said. He raised his glass as Ben picked his back up quickly. They both took another sip. Whenever one of them said *I'll drink to that,* they would always have to have a sip of their drink. And, if they didn't have a drink in front of them when it was said, they would have to both get one. They both placed their glasses on the bar. The bartender walked through a door behind the bar; obviously to check something out the back. "When we were in Hell, Lucifer said something to me," Ben said.

"What's that?" Marcus asked.

Ben rotated in his chair to face Marcus. "Just before he attacked me, whilst you were making your sword, he said that when you started drinking, you let your guard down. What did he mean by that?"

Marcus sat staring at his reflection in the mirror behind the bar. He began to speak. "I used to have a friend called Percy," he started, "a demon."

"Wait," Ben interrupted, "you were actually friends with a demon?"

"Yes, close friends actually. He was to me, like you are to me now. He was good natured and desperately wanted to become an angel. And, he had a slight charm about him. Everyone he met just seemed to like him. I taught him everything I know about fighting; except for one thing that he always wanted to learn. He was funny, too. We got along like a house on fire. That joke I've always said about feathers being so angelic..."

"Yeah?" Ben asked.

"He used to think it was hilarious. At least somebody did. We started going to these tournaments. Angels versus demons."

"Yes, Lucifer mentioned those. He said you were unbeaten," Ben said.

"I *was* unbeaten. He probably didn't mention that, did he?"

"Well, he did try to kill me, didn't he?"

"Yes, good point," Marcus said. "So anyhow, Percy and I started drinking a lot and going to these tournaments. We used to win every single fight. Then, he did something worse than stabbing me in the back, he stabbed me in the front. I could never call him a coward. He didn't go behind my back. He did it straight in front of me."

"What did he do?" Ben asked.

"After a lot of whiskey and fighting, he starts to talk about me being the undefeated champion, and that surely I can beat every single demon in the room with one hand tied behind my back. Sure enough, my hand was grabbed from behind and tied behind my back. Percy was the first to jump at me. I pushed him away, thinking he was joking, but they all started piling on top of me, kicking and punching and stabbing. He called out that I'd had enough and they all got up off of me. I tried to stand up and just barely made it to my feet. He had this glimpse of victory in his eyes. 'Now, I'm the undefeated champion,' he said."

Marcus took another sip of his drink. "I stood there with rage in my eyes, wondering how Percy could have possibly enjoyed that. Friends don't do that to each other. Then, he said something I'll never forget."

"What's that?" Ben asked, with his eyes wide open.

"Kill him," Marcus said.

Ben opened his eyelids as wide as they would go, without his eyes falling out of his head. He stared at Marcus almost in disbelief. "That stuff that Baal used to bind us at your house?" Marcus asked, "what was it?"

"Devil's rope," Marcus said. "It can bind anything; even devils themselves. I guess the best way to describe it is that it's cursed, like your staff is blessed. Nothing can get out of its binds."

"But you broke out of it at my house," Ben said.

"How do you think I learned how to do that?" Marcus asked.

Ben pictured Marcus' story with Percy in his head. Marcus standing there with one arm tied behind his back; a whole bunch of demons and angels standing around him in a circle. "Why didn't the angels help you?" Ben asked.

"They left. Felt they couldn't save me," Marcus replied as he took another sip. Ben took the cue and picked up his glass, and took his own sip. "How did they tie your arm behind your back?"

"They wrapped the devils rope around my stomach with my arm wrenched as far as it would go behind my back. While I was standing there, drunk and bloody with demons advancing on me, I channeled all the strength in my body into that one arm, and ripped it away from my body. The devils rope practically exploded off of me, and everyone stepped back. I knelt down and began to pray quietly. Percy shouted at the group of demons again to kill me, as I knelt there with my fists at my forehead. I stood up and fought harder than I have ever fought before. They just kept coming at me, from every direction. I lost count of how many I killed. Eventually, it was just Percy and I standing there, by ourselves, in a floor of corpses."

Ben turned back to the bar and took another sip of his drink. He looked at Marcus and noticed that he was still staring at his reflection. Anger was in his eyes, and his stare showed that he was remembering every little detail and seeing it all over again in his head. "How did you kill him?" Ben asked.

"What makes you think I killed him?" Marcus asked back.

"Come on, it's you. You probably sliced him in half or something," Ben said.

"Percy's End," Marcus said.

"Wait." Ben sat up straight. "That's the name of something you taught me."

"And it's something he'll never know how to do," Marcus said, as he lifted one side of his mouth into a half smile. "And, yes, he ended up in two pieces."

Ben laughed. "You named it after him. That's hilarious. So, you never taught him that?"
"What use would a demon have for it? You gotta pray first. Demons don't pray," Marcus said.

"To be honest, when you taught me, I didn't even think it was really possible to punch through a body, but I just went along with it anyway. You must have used some real force," Ben said.

"That's why you pray. If you ask God to give you strength, he gives it to you. Whether it's strength to live another day, or the strength to get off drugs, or to find a job. He gives it to you. Do you think anyone thanks him afterwards? Not many people. Once they've actually achieved what it was they set out to do, who takes the credit? They do."

"Thank you," Ben said.

"What for?" Marcus asked.

"For giving me the strength to do this with you. This journey is the most amazing thing I've ever experienced, and downright the most fucked up thing I've ever experienced.

You've just... you've made it look so easy, and you've coached me through everything."

"It's not me you should be thanking for the strength to get through this," Marcus said.

Ben looked down at his drink, and then up at the roof. "Thank you," he said to the ceiling.
"That's better," Marcus said.

They heard cautious footsteps coming up behind them. It was Azazel. He had his finger to his mouth. He pointed to the door behind the bar and then beckoned them to follow him back to the rooms. Marcus and Ben both finished their drinks and quietly stood up and followed him. They both looked through the door behind the bar and saw the bartender lying on his back. They clicked on very quickly. Marcus dashed to the bar and grabbed the bottle of Johnnie Walker Blue and then the three of them ran back to room 6. The door opened quickly. "Come on, hurry up," Lucifer whispered, as he held the door open. They piled into the room one by one, and turned to look at Lucifer. "What's going on?" Marcus asked.

"We've got company," Lucifer said. He pointed out the large window at the end of the room, which was overlooking the beach. There were masses of people standing very still on the beach, and staring straight at them. Marcus popped the cork lid off the bottle and took a swig. He handed the bottle to Ben who took it reluctantly. "Oh, look at you two," Lucifer said. "We're slightly in the middle of a crisis and you're drinking. Give me that." He grabbed the bottle and took a large gulp.

"Hey, the bartender's dead. He ain't gonna miss it."

"Any ideas?" Lucifer asked, wiping his mouth.

"Yeah," Marcus said, "give me your sword."
Lucifer looked at Marcus with confusion in his eyes. He reached behind him and under his jacket, and handed Marcus his sword. Marcus reached under his own jacket and pulled his own sword out. He held one in each hand and held them out at his sides to his arms extent. He threw his arms together in front of him and the swords made a loud clang. They both began glowing furiously. They became one sword. The glow from the blade was a bright white, like burning magnesium. It was harsh to look at. "Wings," Marcus said. "I can guarantee there are no humans about." The four of them let their wings shoot out of their backs. The four different colours of blue, gold, white and black merged in the room.

Ben looked out the window at the hundreds of people standing on the beach. It was raining hard, and they were all soaked to the skin, with their hair plastered to their faces. "If they're not humans," he said, "what are they?"

"Possessed," Azazel said.

"Where are we going?" Lucifer asked.

"You two go out and up, and get Ben to safety beyond the trees," Marcus replied. "Azazel, follow me, I know this place." Lucifer put the bottle on the wall unit to the side of the room. Marcus launched himself at the window. He burst through it, shattering the entire pane of glass. Shards rained all over the outside, as the other three closed their eyes and flew out behind Marcus. Ben and Lucifer reopened their eyes and flew up. Marcus' blue wings and the bright white sword were ahead of them, surrounded by a black sky covered with stars. Ben was smiling as he was flying. He was keeping up, and felt confident about his flying now. Marcus changed direction and started flying back towards the ground. He was moving like a bullet, changing his direction like a ricochet. Azazel followed him almost perfectly. They both landed on the ground amid the bodies of people, who began rushing toward them, like a hungry mob of zombies. The sword in Marcus' hand glowed furiously and swung all around him with precision, cutting them all down in seconds. Azazel used his brute force. His limbs flailing about like large tree trunks, knocking everything senseless. Bones broke, blood spattered, and grey cement-like liquid began to flow as they were killed. Azazel had a slight grin at the fact that he was fighting side by side with Marcus. He felt so close to becoming an angel again, and he could feel the good running through him. He missed the sense of purposefulness.

Shunk...

It was a miracle they both heard it. Azazel threw the body he was grappling with at Marcus, who sliced it in two with the sword as they both leaned backwards to avoid the hulking mass with his blade swiping directly between them. Orias landed and turned around to face them both, as they were surrounded by demons. The rain continued to pour as they stood staring at each other. Eligos landed next to Orias as

Marcus took a step back. Azazel noticed it. He looked at Marcus. "Let me take her, Lucifer told me. You take the big one!" Marcus nodded.

Marcus darted toward Orias in a flash of blue. His right shoulder was wound right back and his arm began shooting forward, the closer he got. A heavily telegraphed punch, but at the speed Marcus was moving, Orias didn't have a chance. It hit him swiftly and powerful on the left cheek as he went down. He quickly got back up and the two engaged in a furious fist fight. Azazel sidestepped around Eligos. He knew her well and knew she wouldn't be easy to take down. She matched his sidestep. "Now Azazel, do you really think your brute strength is going to stop me?"

Azazel smirked. "As long as I keep away from your lips, I think so." Azazel ran at her and went into a slide, as a blue mist came from her lips. It just missed him as he tackled her feet and caught her by surprise. She went down as Azazel grabbed her legs and began contorting them into a position he could manipulate. He was excellent with grapples and holds, and was certain that this was the best way to beat her. She was face down as he had his leg on her thighs, and was bending her ankles down towards her spine. Her torso began to rotate despite her legs, like a grotesque spineless creature that could rotate any body part in any direction. She lunged forward and wrapped her arms around Azazel's neck as he let go of her legs, and she stood up, subduing him as easily as anything. Marcus noticed from behind her as he was focusing on Orias, who swung a large wound up punch Marcus could see a mile away. Marcus ducked as Orias swung forward and was thrown off balance with the momentum of his punch, to the point that his left leg was lifted a little off the ground. Marcus saw the opportunity. He took it. The ground was so slick with the rain that he was able to slide across the ground underneath Orias, and grabbed his left leg that was partially off the ground. He used Orias' momentum against him as he used all his strength to begin swinging him around and around. Marcus was spinning in circles with Orias' leg firmly in his hands and flailing about like a hammer toss. Marcus was struggling, but was able to maintain the spin as he edged closer to Eligos and Azazel, who both had their backs to Marcus and Orias; Eligos still with her arms around Azazel's neck. "Hey bitch face!" Marcus called.

Eligos grimaced in anger and let go of Azazel to focus on Marcus. Azazel broke free and turned to see Marcus in the spin, with Orias swinging around him. He clued on very quickly and ran as far from Eligos as he could. Eligos saw what Marcus was doing and was about to flee, when Marcus let go of the behemoth, just as he was almost facing her. Orias hurtled toward her with such force that when they collided with a loud thud, they both went tumbling off into the distance. The other demons fled. "Shunk!" Marcus yelled, as they collided with his arms outstretched. Azazel threw his arm around Marcus in triumph, as they both let out cries out joy. "That was good," Azazel said.

"I know, right?"

"Quite an arm you've got there." They both laughed as they flew off into the sky. They flew towards what looked like a forest, and ploughed through the trees to where Ben and Lucifer were. Marcus let his wings seep down into his back, and the others followed suit. He walked over to a small body of water that in the darkness, looked like it merged through the trees into a lake. Marcus put the sword in the water and it hissed loudly. He pulled it out and the bright light was extinguished, as he flipped the sword in his hand to hold the blade and handed the sword to Lucifer. "Okay, they'll be guarding the entire waterfront, no doubt. I don't know how they found us," Marcus said.

"I can probably answer that," a familiar voice said in the darkness. Asmodeus came out from behind a tree. "Look at you all. So desperate to get this sword and go into battle. Don't you understand? You've already lost," Asmodeus said. "Lucifer, you're so blinded by the light that you think he'll just let you walk back into Heaven. Azazel, you know you won't even get a sniff of the place. Look at the two little angels."

"Right!" Azazel shouted. "I've 'ad enough of you, ya bleedin' tosser. Give me a knife!" Ben handed Marcus' dagger to Azazel, who walked towards Asmodeus. He held it firmly by his side in his oversized hand as he walked. A sword appeared in Asmodeus' hand and he thrust it forward, stabbing Azazel straight through the chest. Azazel gasped and dropped Marcus' dagger at his feet. He staggered like he was drunk and then burst into the pasty cement like liquid. Asmodeus circled around the puddle on the ground towards Lucifer. Ben circled around away from him and towards the puddle.

"So, you're tired of ruling in Hell, is that it? You can't stand it any longer? What's gotten into you? You've gone all bloody goody good on me with a drunken angel and his little human friend. I'm taking over Hell, and you can say goodbye." Ben knelt down and put his fists to his head. Asmodeus turned and looked at him. "What are you doing?" he asked Ben.

Ben looked up from behind his fists. "I'm praying," he said smugly.

"Well it won't help you. Not even God can stop me now."

Asmodeus turned back to Lucifer and lifted up his sword. "Say goodbye, dear friend." Asmodeus closed his eyes and swung his sword towards Lucifer, but it was stopped suddenly with a loud clang. He opened his eyes and looked down the blade of his sword to see Marcus standing in front of Lucifer with his arm up over his head. The sword had hit the cuff around Marcus' wrist which was now glowing bright white. The fire in Marcus' eyes burned. Asmodeus chuckled. "You? What are you going to do? You don't even have a sword," he said. Marcus thrust his arm up, pushing the sword away, and kicked Asmodeus in the stomach. Asmodeus stepped back in pain. "I don't need one," Marcus said.

Ben slowly reached down and wrapped his hand around the handle of Marcus' dagger, which was laying by the puddle where Azazel was killed. He was still praying. Asmodeus stepped forward and swung the sword at Marcus, who stepped back to dodge while Asmodeus corrected and came back with another swing. Marcus stepped to the side and flung his leg up and back, kicking Asmodeus in the face. Asmodeus stumbled backwards and regained his balance as he came at Marcus again. "Marcus!" Ben shouted, as he threw the dagger. Marcus caught it by the handle and held it up to deflect Asmodeus' sword. Asmodeus corrected and swung the sword from the side. Marcus stepped back and pointed the dagger towards the ground. The sword hit the dagger with a loud *chink* noise. Asmodeus stepped back and assessed the situation. He raised the sword behind his head with both hands and swung a massive blow forward. Marcus ducked and speared himself under the swing and towards Asmodeus' stomach. He reversed the dagger in his hand and put the palm of his other hand on the very tip of the handle for more force. He thrust the dagger up and into Asmodeus' stomach. Asmodeus gasped. Marcus rotated the dagger inside the wound and Asmodeus dropped the sword. "You killed my friend," Marcus said.

Marcus ripped the dagger out, causing more damage to the wound with the barbs on the blade, and he stepped back. Asmodeus burst into the same cement-like paste as Azazel. Marcus was breathing heavily. He grabbed Lucifer by the shirt and pulled him in close. "I have a plan," he said.

CHAPTER VII

"Ben, where is your staff?" Marcus asked. Ben touched his shoulder in realisation that it wasn't there. A new sense of fear hit his eyes. "It's at the hotel," he replied.

"Okay, you two, wait here. I'll go get it." Marcus was instantly standing in room 5 at the Kuwait Hilton Resort, facing the door. He looked next to the bed closest to the door and saw the staff lying on the floor. He breathed a sigh of relief. He bent down and picked it up and turned around to face the window. He jumped back in shock. There were blank expressionless faces standing just outside the window, with masses of faces behind them. Beyond them, he saw Orias and Eligos. He heard the door open and the bartender he had earlier seen lying on the floor behind the bar, walked into the room. His eyes showed nothing. Marcus disappeared.

He reappeared in the clearing where Ben and Lucifer were standing. He had a look of shock in his eyes and his body language was showing that he was slightly discomforted. "Marcus, are you okay?" Ben asked.

Marcus threw the staff to Ben. "Whatever you do," he said, "don't go back to the hotel. They're everywhere!"

"So, what is this plan?" Lucifer asked.

"Okay," Marcus said, "Lucifer, when you bought the boat, did you have a look inside at all?"

"Of course, I did. Do you think I'm stupid?" Lucifer asked.

"Just checking. Okay, does it have a cabin?"

"With four beds and all. Why?"

"I need you to take Ben with you, and transport inside the cabin. You will need to start the engine and get ready to sail. Ben, I want you to take out anything that tries to get on board."

"What if there's too many of them?" Ben asked.

"There won't be. They'll be too distracted," Marcus said.

"By what?" Lucifer asked.

"I'll handle the distraction. You two just get the boat going and make sure nobody gets on," Marcus said.

"What about you?" Ben asked. "Will you make it to the boat?"

"I'll get there," Marcus said. "Where on the waterfront is the boat?"

"It's right near the ornamental pool," Lucifer said.

"I was hoping you'd say that. I need you to get clear of the promenade. They'll be everywhere. I'm going to need that sword back," Marcus said.

Lucifer handed the sword to Marcus who let it disappear as he put it up under his jacket. "What are you going to do?" Lucifer asked.

Marcus put his hand under his t-shirt just below his neck and pulled out the cross he took from his apartment. He stroked it with his thumb. "I'll improvise," he said. "Don't start the boat until they're completely away from the dock. Go!"

Lucifer and Ben were standing in the dark. Ben put his hand in his pocket and pulled out a chrome lighter. He flicked it open and thumbed the wheel. It lit up the cabin of Lucifer's boat. Lucifer walked up two steps to the door and quietly pulled it open. He stepped out onto the deck and Ben followed. They crouched low and looked over the edge of the boat. The waterfront was covered with people surrounding a large rectangular pool of water, with a series of lights winding down the middle of it like a snake. They curved around and formed a big circle of lights nearer the docks. There was water spurting out of the pool where the lights were. The people surrounding the pool were all looking up to the sky. Lucifer and Ben followed their gazes and saw Marcus' blue wings in the dark sky, fifty feet above the pool. His wings were swaying slowly in the wind.

Marcus was holding the cross in his right hand, with the chain dangling out of his fist. He had his left hand cupped behind his right and they were both up just below his chin. There was a cigarette in between two fingers of his left hand. He was quietly praying with his eyes closed. He opened his eyes and dropped the cross. It twirled in the air and fell into the ornamental pool below him. He let himself fall the fifty feet to the pool below, and landed in it with a large splash. The crowd of people surrounding the pool jumped in after him. Smoke started rising from their bodies as they fell into the water, one by one. They all started screaming in pain and began bursting. The water turned grey and Marcus leaped out of the water. He landed on the side of the pool, drenched in holy water, which trickled down his face. His hair was plastered to his cheeks and almost framed his face perfectly. Ben and Lucifer stared from the side of the boat. "What's going on?" Ben whispered.

"He blessed the water with the cross, and now that he's drenched in it, they shouldn't be able to touch him without getting hurt," Lucifer whispered back.

The people closest to the boat swarmed towards Marcus. Lucifer stood up and walked over to the controls of the boat. He pulled a set of keys out of his pocket and put them into the ignition. He started the boat. Ben stood up and pulled his bow staff off his shoulder, ready to take on anything that came at him. Marcus slowly started walking towards the boat. He pulled the sword out from under his jacket and walked straight through the masses of people. They all cowered at the bright light shining from the sword; shielding their eyes. One of them ran at him and Marcus quickly ducked. The man fell on top of him and he thrust his whole body upward, flipping the man off of him. He brought his sword around and stabbed the man through the stomach. The man burst and fell into a puddle behind Marcus as he kept walking. Ben watched in awe as Marcus stormed through the crowd. One of the crowd turned around and saw Ben standing on the boat with his staff. The man quickly ran towards the boat and leaped onto the back of it. Ben hit him in the head with the bow staff. The crowd turned around to see what was going on, and began rushing towards the boat. Marcus flew up out of the middle of them and landed on the dock, just behind the boat. "Go!" he shouted to them.

He raised his sword and swung it at the first man. The sword sliced him clean in half before he burst. Marcus swung his sword around backhand and hit another one. Ben was standing ready, in case any of them got past him. Orias began running through the crowd, knocking the mindless drones out of the way as he rushed toward Marcus. The edge of the dock was covered in the grey cement-like liquid as Marcus kept flailing about with his sword, expertly slicing everything that came within his proximity. He saw Orias advancing and flew up quickly and landed next to the pool. The demons changed direction and headed for him, as well as Orias, who kept swatting them out of his way to reach his prize. He came close as Marcus swung toward him and deflected the blow with his dagger. The rest of the demons backed off, letting Orias take charge, as he and Marcus locked blades.

Marcus, with his sword in two hands, and Orias with his dagger in his right, below the knuckles, and his stone in his left. He sliced furiously at Marcus with such speed it almost caught Marcus off guard. He deflected with the sword and jumped back to avoid being sliced, until he was able to finally get a hit in. He swung swiftly at Orias' hand and the sword caught him on the wrist, slicing his hand clean off. Orias bellowed in pain and anger as he came harder and faster at Marcus with the stone in his left hand. Marcus let his sword disappear as he dodged the powerful blows. Orias lunged at Marcus and used his entire body weight to knock Marcus down.

They fell to the ground with a loud thud - Orias on top of Marcus - pinning him with his weight, as his right wounded arm touched the water in the pool. The holy water burned his arm and almost cauterized his wound, as he arched his back up and lifted his left arm to start bludgeoning Marcus. The stone in his hand came down with a colossal force as Marcus struggled to lean left and right to avoid the blows. Orias kept on smashing his stone down toward Marcus like an oversized caveman, as Marcus was eventually able to block. He brought both of his arms up and crossed them at the wrists to block the blow, and as Orias' arm came down and fell perfectly into the gap between Marcus' wrists, Marcus latched on with all his might, and then twisted. It was a move he'd used so many times before. In one swift twist, he was able to bend Orias' hand back against his own arm, and hold him without too much effort. An arm bar, they call it. Used properly, you can pretty much make your aggressor move any way you want them to. Marcus lifted Orias' arm up enough to be able to squirm out from underneath, and maintain the hold. Orias swung his cauterized stump at Marcus, which hit him on the side of the head and knocked him off balance. He lost his grip on the arm bar, and was turned around by the force of the blow. Orias grabbed him from behind in a bear hug.

Lucifer pushed the throttle forward and the bow rose out of the water. The boat began to take off. He edged it out of the dock and towards the gap in the promenade. The two piers ran out from each edge of the complex and out into the water with a large gap for boats to get through. The piers were covered in people. Lucifer gunned the motor as hard as it would go, as the bow of the boat lifted even higher. People started jumping off the pier in anticipation to jump on the boat, as Ben stepped backward towards the cabin. They reached the gap in between the piers and Ben saw Marcus in the distance, struggling with Orias. He almost didn't notice the hands coming up onto the side of the boat.

Marcus struggled in Orias' grasp, and bucked and thrashed against him, as Orias squeezed harder. Marcus almost felt helpless, but with every fibre of his being, he leaned forward as far as he could, and snapped his head back as fast as he could move. The top of his head hit Orias squarely on the jaw, who began to fall backward, into the pool, with Marcus still clutched in his arms. They landed in the water with a large splash, as Marcus fought free. He fought his way to the side and clambered up out of the water, drenched again in holy water and Purgatory sludge. His blue wings seeped out of his back, as he heard the noise behind him of Orias emerging from the water, and hoisting himself up onto the side of the pool. His skin was melted by the holy water and his rugged good looks were now a gruesome mess. His one good arm held him up on the side of the pool - still clutching his precious stone - whilst his right arm hung lifeless from his side. Marcus reached under his jacket and pulled out the sword again, as he grabbed Orias by the hair and lifted him up into the air. The world around them changed as Purgatory erupted into view. Marcus transported them both there so that he could finally do away with the large beast. He looked down at Orias who struggled to free Marcus' grip on his hair with his good hand, while Marcus readied his sword and pulled Orias up to his level. They were floating high above the ground in Purgatory, and Orias' weight was now just a melted mess. Marcus swung the sword, slicing Orias' head clean off as his body burst into flames on its decline. Marcus let go of the head, and let it burst into flames as it fell.

Ben swung his staff around and smashed it against one of the hands that were coming up onto the side of the boat. He heard a scream, and quickly spun his staff around to hit the other hand. The man on the side of the boat fell off. People started jumping at the boat and grabbing onto the sides. Ben swung his staff above his head, and starting batting them off like flies. He was very skilled with his staff, and as the people started climbing up onto the side of the boat, he didn't hesitate. Ben just knocked them off with every swing. They were coming at him from all angles. He quickly glanced towards the ornamental pool and couldn't see Marcus anymore. At that moment, one woman had climbed up onto the back of the boat and came tumbling towards Ben. She tackled him to the floor and he fought to get her off of him.

Marcus reappeared back above the ornamental pool and floated down to the ground. The demons were gone, and most likely focusing their efforts on the boat. Marcus bent down and picked up Orias' dagger, which was lying there on the ground, covered in the grey liquid. He picked it up as Eligos crept up behind him. He turned to face her, and held up the dagger. "Spoils of war. Unless, you want something to remember him by."

She scowled. "This doesn't prove anything," she said.

"It proves something. If he can be killed, so can you. It won't be by my hand, but I can guarantee you, it will happen."

Eligos smirked. "Best you protect that boy. He is the descendant of Amalie, is he not? The bloodline everyone has been looking for."

Marcus opened his eyes wide. "How did you know?"

Her smirk changed to a sultry look. "I can smell it in his blood. He is the first born of the first born. The blood of angels flows through his veins."

"You stay away from him!"

Eligos began to walk backwards. "By all means, try and stop me." Marcus took a step forward. "Keep the blade. It means nothing to me."

Eligos disappeared in a cloud of black smoke. Marcus inspected the dagger closely. It was a greyish colour, with a textured curved handle; easy to hold below the knuckles, and the blade itself was arced, almost like a small scimitar. It was as sharp as a razor blade; well used, but very sharp. Marcus let it disappear in his hand. He had an arsenal of weapons in a secret room behind the bookshelf in his apartment. Angels were able to transport their weapons to and from a safe location. It's how Marcus had made his weapons disappear, and reappear. The dagger was now added to his collection. He smirked a little and looked out over the water, attempting to see the boat.

Ben struggled as the woman on top of him was trying to scratch at him and bite him. She was somehow pulled away from him, and started flying backwards. She fell into the water like she had been thrown. Ben looked up and saw Marcus standing above him. "Hope I'm not too late," he said. He helped Ben up, and they put their backs to each other; a common stance they had rehearsed in many previous fights. The boat was clear, and the people left on the piers were still leaping off to reach the boat, but were falling short. "Faster!" Marcus yelled to Lucifer. Lucifer pushed it to full throttle, and Marcus and Ben stepped sideways to correct for the acceleration. The front of the boat lifted out of the water as they made their way out into the Persian Gulf.

Lucifer set it back to a slow cruise, and turned in his chair to look at Marcus. He was sitting to the side of the boat with his head resting back against the side, and his legs spread out. Ben came out from the cabin underneath the front of the boat with some blankets. He gave one to Marcus, and threw one around himself. He walked over to the wheel where Lucifer was sitting, and looked out to the open waters. "Are we heading in the right direction?" he asked.

"We will be as soon as Marcus gives me the coordinates," Lucifer replied. They both turned to look at Marcus. He had the blanket on top of him and was fast asleep. "Marcus!" Lucifer shouted.

Marcus woke up and looked a little dazed. He looked around him at his surroundings, and then at Ben and Lucifer. "What?" he asked.

"Where are we going?" Lucifer asked.

"Head for Iran," Marcus said. "From what I've researched, it's near the head of the Gulf." He took the blanket off, stood up, and pulled the notebook out of his inside jacket pocket. He unlatched it and opened it up to a specific page. He walked over to the light from the console and inspected the page thoroughly. "Okay, go north-east. We should be there by sun up." He closed the notebook and put it back inside his jacket. Ben looked at Marcus and noticed he was exhausted. "I saw you fighting that big one. What happened?"

Marcus exhaled. "Orias is dead."

Lucifer turned around in his chair and stared at Marcus. "Eligos?" he asked, hopefully.

Marcus shook his head. "No doubt, we will see her again."

He walked through the door leading into the cabin and closed it behind him. He lay down on one of the beds and closed his eyes. He opened them again not long after, as he heard Ben and Lucifer talking loudly above his head. He walked up onto the deck to see what the fuss was about. The sun was just coming up and they could see land in the far distance. Ben and Lucifer were intently looking at the front of the boat. Marcus looked to where their eyes were fixed and he saw a bird standing on the front of the boat with a twig in its' mouth. Marcus opened his eyes wide. "Stop the boat," he said.

Lucifer and Ben both turned around to look at him. "Why?" Lucifer asked.

"Because we're here," Marcus replied.

Lucifer brought the boat to a stop and turned his body half around in his chair to look at Marcus. "How do you know?" he asked.

Marcus pointed at the bird. "A little birdy told me," he said.

Lucifer looked at the bird in confusion, and suddenly clicked. "How is that of any relevance?"

"Divine intervention?" Marcus replied.

Lucifer shrugged in a skeptical acceptance, as Ben walked to the back of the boat and looked at the water. There was a small whirlpool just behind the boat. It started growing bigger. "Uh, guys?" Ben said.

Marcus and Lucifer walked to where Ben was standing, and looked at the whirlpool. It was growing bigger by the second. Both Marcus and Lucifer looked at Ben. He took his eyes off the whirlpool and looked back at them. They both looked at his staff. "Oh, right," he said, as he took his staff off his shoulder. Ben stood at the very edge of the boat and held his staff up in his right hand. He held it out over the water and the whirlpool began to get a whole lot deeper. He put his left hand up and started moving his hands away from each other, as if he was physically trying to separate the water. The whirlpool grew in diameter instantly, and the boat started to tip into it. Ben stood frozen with shock.

"We're going to go under!" Lucifer shouted over the raging water.

"That's the idea!" Marcus shouted back.

The boat started spinning sideways in the current, doing complete circles around the maelstrom. The current started moving faster as the boat moved towards the centre. The boat was practically vertical while Ben and Lucifer shuffled upwards, towards the cabin. They were holding onto the sides of the boat, fighting to stay aboard. Marcus was still standing at the end of the boat, but standing on the edge keeping himself vertical. The boat slipped under. Water piled on top of them and they lost their grip. They started swirling around in the watery hurricane, kicking to reach the surface, all whilst trying to avoid the boat that was flying around them in the current at great speed. All except Marcus, who was fighting the current to swim downwards.

The water pulled Ben and Lucifer down to where Marcus was, as the three of them kicked and kicked to gain some kind of direction. The sky was gone and they were surrounded by water in every direction. The speed of the water had died down, and as they began floating and looking around in every direction, they noticed that the boat seemed to be floating upward. They realised they were upside down. Ben still had a firm hold of his staff. Marcus spotted a small light in the distance, and began swimming towards it. The other two followed him as he kicked his legs violently to gain more speed. He reached the surface and took a long gasp, as Ben and Lucifer launched out of the water. The three of them all looked at each other. Marcus felt soft sand under his feet, and then looked above Ben and Lucifer's' heads in awe. Ben and Lucifer turned around to see what Marcus was looking at. There was a beach with trees all along it. Marcus staggered through the water, up towards the beach. As he stood on the beach, he peered out over the water to see where they were. All he saw was water all the way to the horizon. He turned around and looked at the trees beyond the beach. Lucifer and Ben came out of the water "Where are we?" Ben asked.

"Must have washed ashore somewhere in the Gulf. Maybe a small island somewhere," Lucifer replied.

"We can't be," Marcus said. "There's no other land in sight."

"So, what do we do?" Ben asked.

"We walk. There's got to be some sort of civilization here," Marcus replied.

They walked to the trees and tried to find a viable way through. Marcus pulled out the sword and started hacking away at the small branches that were in the way. They found a small opening and stopped to have a rest. Marcus sat on a large rock sticking out of the ground, and Ben lay down on the grass. Lucifer was standing up and looking around.

"What is it?" Marcus asked.

"This all looks familiar," Lucifer said. "I've seen this place before."

Marcus looked around and stood up. He recognised the clearing almost instantly. "Of course, it looks familiar. This is Hell."

Ben looked up at the two of them in shock. "This is Hell?" he asked.

"Not exactly," Lucifer said. "It's outside the gates."

Lucifer kept looking around at the trees surrounding them. His eyes tracked all the way around from the path Marcus had cut through for them from the beach, to the other side of the clearing. It seemed to narrow near the end, and petered out into a path. As the path wove through the trees, the blacker it became, and a gradient of lush trees to ash sprawled out in front of them. Lucifer saw the Gates of Hell beyond the trees, far in the distance. "Look!" he said. "There's the gates."

"You know what that means, don't you?" Marcus said.

"Well, by the glow of your pendant, and by being in this clearing, I'd say we're nearly there," Lucifer said.

Ben stood up and looked at the gates. He noticed Hell beyond them as he saw it before, and gave Marcus and Lucifer a queried look. He noticed the gates were really just a gigantic stone archway, with no doors, and no guards. He became annoyed. "You mean all this time, all we needed to do to get here, was walk out the Gates of Hell?"

Marcus and Lucifer shifted their gaze towards Ben. Lucifer looked horrified. "Are you mad?" Lucifer asked.

Ben held his hands up as a question and raised half his top lip in a stupefied gesture. "We had to go to England, and come to Kuwait, go through that whole hotel incident, not to mention the waterfront incident, then fall into a maelstrom. When, all we had to do was walk out the damn Gates of Hell! Why didn't we just do that?"

Marcus and Lucifer both sighed. "Cerberus," they both said.

They heard a loud screeching in the distance, that sounded like more than one creature. "Cerberus? The three-headed dog? That thing is *real*?"

"Oh, he's very real. And very quick to temper," Lucifer said.

"He's also not a dog," Marcus added.

Ben was still confused. "But they're the Gates of Hell. Surely you two can pass by him? Isn't that the entrance?"

"Far from it!" Lucifer remarked. "It's the exit. Think about it. You're in Hell, you can see an empty Paradise sitting just in the distance, the gate is open, and seemingly unguarded. Maybe you can make it. You try, and the beast shows himself. It's there, purely to make the damned think they can escape. No one goes near the gate. Not even us."

"You can't transport past it?" Ben asked.

"Outside the gates is off limits to anyone, for obvious reasons. No one comes out here, but the beast. Trust me, we came the safe way, and he had to hide it somewhere. We haven't been able to see it in a long while. All this time I thought he'd moved it."

Ben put his hands up in submission. "Okay, I guess I should listen to you guys. I am the rookie, after all. All this way, just to get outside the damn gates."

Marcus walked around the tree line to where the trees started to turn to ash. "This way," Marcus said. He found an opening in the clearing, which almost resembled a dirt path. It wound back through the green lush trees and away from the Gates of Hell. They began to make their way along it with ease, as it wasn't quite as dense as the path they had to cut through to get to the clearing. It looked like it had been made by thousands of footprints over time. Marcus looked closer at the ground, and noticed that some of the footprints were a little fresher than they should be; almost as if someone had been there recently. "This can't be right," Marcus said. "These footprints look a day or two old."

They continued to walk, as the path seemed to go uphill, and they noticed the incline with each step getting harder. Ben kept his eyes looking around at the trees, concerned about the footprints. He was at the back, and Lucifer was in the middle, keeping his eyes on his feet, plodding along, occasionally glancing at Marcus' feet in front of him, to make sure he was still following him. Marcus kept his determination in his eyes as he scanned all around him. He saw the top getting closer, and figured they could take a look around and rest. As he reached the top, his eyes wandered down the path and down the hill, and stopped at the end. In the distance, at the end of the path, he saw another clearing, and at the far end, the trees formed a thick tree line. There was a gap; an opening in the trees. It looked like it opened out into a luscious green valley, with the tips of the trees either side joining in the middle, forming an archway. In the very middle of the opening, he saw a sword. It was a large sword with a big handle. The blade was sharp on both sides, and the flat of the blade was as flat as they come. The sword opened up into two small barbs at the end of the blade near the handle; one of which was broken off, and the hilt was shaped like Marcus' wings, only they were gold. The blade was on fire. Night was falling, which made the sword stand out even more. Ben and Lucifer looked at it with a great sense of satisfaction.

Marcus stood up slowly, still staring at his sword. He began to walk towards it. He didn't notice the tip of the spear just below his chin. He stopped when a whole bunch of spears were pointing directly at his face. He looked around as best as he could without being cut by one of them, and saw a tribe of people standing all around them. In front of him, they began to part and form a walkway. A big man walked down the pathway towards Marcus. He stopped directly in front of him. "Only angels may pass here." The big man said in perfect English.

Marcus looked all around him and then thrust his wings out of his shoulders. The big man looked up in awe at the blue wings. Ben and Lucifer opened up their wings as well. The entire tribe in front of them began to kneel. The big man who was obviously some sort of chief, stood back up. "Marcus," he said, "take what belongs to you."

The man stood aside, and Marcus walked down the hill into the clearing. Two angels appeared on either side of the sword. They looked at Marcus and nodded. They were cherubs, like he was. Their blue wings were swaying in the breeze. Marcus looked at the two of them, and at his sword. He turned around and walked back to Ben and Lucifer. "We go in at dawn," he said.

They sat down with the tribe and talked through the night. The moon was just visible through the treetops, and the conversation changed topics many times. "I'm kinda sad about Azazel. I was actually beginning to like him," Marcus said.

"He took a real shining to you after you killed Baal," Lucifer said. "Twice! There's one devil you won't be seeing again."

Marcus looked at Lucifer. "Hey, you're the devil," he said jokingly.

Ben looked at Marcus in shock. Lucifer began to laugh. They all joined in laughing with him. Lucifer looked at his brother with great respect in his eyes. "I knew you had it in you, Marcus. I knew you would find it. It only took you seven hundred years!" he joked.

"Hey, I'm here, aren't I?" Marcus asked.

"That, you are," Lucifer replied. "That, you are."

They looked up into the night sky. They were all at the end of a long journey. They all knew it was the beginning, but none of them said it. They were all satisfied with their accomplishment. "You've done well, kid," Lucifer said to Ben. Ben looked at Lucifer with a half-smile. He was glad that

Lucifer had finally accepted him. "Yeah, but I couldn't have done any of it without help," Ben replied.

"Don't mention it," Lucifer said, as he sat back.

Marcus leaned over to Lucifer. "He wasn't talking about you, dick face."

Ben looked up into the sky. "Thank you," he said quietly.

The sun began shining brightly through the trees. Marcus stood up and stretched. He looked at Ben and Lucifer. "Are you ready?" he asked.

"Go get it," Lucifer said.

Marcus walked up to the opening, and stared at his sword for a long moment. Lucifer and Ben walked up behind him. Marcus reached up under his jacket and pulled out the sword that he'd merged together in the hotel. He handed it to Lucifer. He took a deep breath and reached out with his right hand to touch his sword. He grabbed the large handle in his hand, and the ground started to vibrate beneath them. The flame on the blade doused itself and the sword began to glow furiously. A large beam shot out of the tip of the sword and into the sky. Marcus looked at the blinding sword. It was so bright that he had to close his eyes and look away. There was a bright stripe on the inside of his eyelids from looking at the it. He opened his eyes and tried to regain focus. The beam in the sky shrank down into the sword, and Marcus pulled it away from the entrance. The angels either side both turned to let him walk through. He walked through the archway and Lucifer followed. Ben watched them walk through and smiled. Marcus turned around to Ben. "Are you coming?" he asked.

"I thought humans were never allowed back into Paradise," Ben said.

Marcus looked up at Ben's' wings. "You got wings, don't you?"

Marcus kept walking. Ben looked above him at his wings floating in the air. He ran through the archway after them. They walked up a large hill and when they reached the top, they stopped to look at their surroundings. They were surrounded by luscious green fields and trees. A large river flowed through the garden, with a big waterfall at one end of it. The view was magnificent. At the bottom of the hill, they saw what looked like a stone table with smaller stones set into the ground around it. They looked about the right height to sit on. God was standing just beyond the table. They walked down the hill towards him, with Lucifer almost in a jog. Lucifer walked around the stone table and right up to God. He stood there for a long moment, surprised that he was actually standing in God's presence once again. He threw his arms around God, who in turn put his arms around Lucifer and stroked his back. Lucifer stood back and God brought his arms around to Lucifer's' shoulders. Lucifer looked into God's blue eyes with great sorrow. "I'm sorry," he said.

God put his hand on Lucifer's' cheek. "I forgive you, my Son," God replied.

Marcus smiled. He walked up to God and stood next to Lucifer. God looked at Marcus with content in his eyes. He put his hands on Marcus' shoulders. "I told you that you could do this, didn't I?"

"No," Marcus said. "You said that you *know* I can do this."

"And yet, you did it. There is a lot more that you need to do after this. You have found your sword, and this is only the beginning," God said.

"I know," Marcus replied.

God looked over at Ben who was still in disbelief that they were standing there in the Garden of Eden, talking to God. "Ben, come closer," he said. "You have been a big part of all of this. Don't think you don't deserve any credit."

Ben walked over to God, and stood next to Marcus. God placed his hands on Ben's' shoulders. "They couldn't have done it without you. And, all of your efforts will not go unrewarded. You are welcome in Heaven, and you are now an angel, like your friends. I couldn't think of anyone better to look after this place than you."

"Here? Paradise?" Ben asked.

"He means Earth, stupid," Marcus said.

God looked at Marcus. "And, you need to watch your mouth," he said. "You have a duty to fulfill."

"Yes Sir," Marcus said.

God turned to Lucifer. "You have also done exceedingly well, my Son. I am happy to grant you full access to Heaven."

"Here comes the *but*," Lucifer remarked.

"But, of course, I want you to rule Hell, *for* Heaven. Your efforts there have been good so far, and I don't think anybody else could do it as well as you. Do you agree?"

"Well, I don't see the harm in it," Lucifer said.

Marcus opened his eyes wide. "A great alliance will be formed," he said.

"And, within doing so, I will need the three of you to cleanse Hell. Anyone who opposes us, must suffer the consequences. Anyone who didn't have the chance to learn the truth during their time on Earth, have earned a second chance to learn. I have already set up an army to follow you into Hell. I will see you all in Heaven. Is there anything else?"

Marcus took a deep breath. "Yes," Marcus said. "We couldn't have done this without Azazel. He deserves redemption."

"I can't take him out of Purgatory, if that's what you mean. But I've got other plans for him. It will be known that he was involved, and his name will be redeemed."

"Thank you," Lucifer said to both Marcus and God.

And with that, God disappeared. The three of them stood still in the field. Lucifer sat down, dazed at the stone table. Marcus looked over at him. "Lucifer? How are you doing?" he asked cautiously.

Lucifer looked up at him. "I've been forgiven," he said. "All this time, all I had to do was apologise."

"Not quite," Marcus said. "You helped us. You helped him. If you hadn't have come along with us, this wouldn't have happened."

"Good point," Lucifer said.

"So, why didn't you do it sooner, eh?"

Lucifer smiled. He jumped up and tackled Marcus playfully. The two of them wrestled on the ground. Ben jumped up on the table and thumped the end of his staff on it. "Um, I believe we have some business to attend to," he said.

Marcus and Lucifer looked up at him. They both stood up and stared at him. A terrible fear fell through Ben's' eyes. He knew what was coming. He turned and leaped off the table. Marcus and Lucifer opened their wings and chased after him.

They tackled him to the ground, and when Ben looked up, they were on top of Devils' Tower. Ben looked around him and saw the stairway. He stood up and brushed himself off. He inspected his jeans. "Great, grass stains," he said. "Do you know how hard these things are to get out?"

Marcus laughed. "After the decayed ooze of Purgatory has been on your clothes, you're worried about grass stains?"

Ben and looked at Lucifer, then back at Marcus. "I like these jeans."

Marcus shook his head and laughed it off. He turned to Lucifer. "Are you sure you're ready for this?" he asked.

"As ready as I'll ever be," Lucifer replied.

Marcus pulled out his sword and began to walk up the steps into Heaven. Ben and Lucifer followed. As Marcus reached the top of the stairs, he looked out over the battlefield, and saw the entrance to Purgatory on the other side. He knew that soon enough, he would be standing there fighting for Heaven. He turned around and walked toward the gates. Peter stood up off of his chair and looked at Marcus, Lucifer and Ben. He nodded as they walked past him. The three of them nodded back, and Marcus grabbed hold of the gates.

CHAPTER VIII

Marcus threw the gates of Heaven open, and walked in with Lucifer on his left, and Ben on his right. Heads turned as they walked in. Angels with all assortments of coloured wings were up in the air. The crowd of angels watched them. Lucifer felt slightly uncomfortable. The faces all around started smiling at the three of them. They all started cheering with a new-found sense of hope. Marcus and Lucifer had returned, and Ben had become one of them. They walked slowly down the blue carpet and passed the smiling faces. Ben felt like a warrior, coming home after battle. He stopped himself from smiling, and tried to look as tough as possible. But, he couldn't resist. He smiled and waved.

They reached the steps at the end of the blue carpet. Marcus brought his left hand over to his right and touched the tip of the sword to the blue carpet. He stood there with both hands resting on top of the handle. He looked up the steps towards God, who held out his hand to point behind them. The three of them looked behind them, and saw thousands of angels with swords in their hands, all the way to the gates. Marcus turned around and looked at all of his soldiers. They were ready for battle, and at his command. He held his sword high in the air as the army cheered. Marcus opened his wings and took off towards the gates. Lucifer and Ben followed, and then the horde of angels rose up off the ground and took off after the three of them. They flew out the gates and down the stairs, past Devils' Tower. Marcus swooped around and dove in through the archway in the stone. All the angels followed.

Marcus landed in Hell and ran down the mountain. His sword was shining brightly, and he held it out in front of him. A large beam of light shot out the end, and flooded the path with light. Anything that stood in the light disintegrated to ashes. Ben was amazed at how powerful the sword really was. Lucifer flew up into the air and looked around Hell. He saw suffering humans everywhere. He flew down and helped out as many as he could, while the rest of the angels battled the demons. He looked back at Marcus and Ben, and saw an unstoppable fighting duo. The two of them had their backs to each other, with Marcus flailing his sword in every direction; cutting demons down where they stood, and Ben was twirling his staff and knocking them about. The swarm of angels flew in over the top and zipped to the ground; their swords slicing through anything that moved. Lucifer got back to his task. He rounded up all the humans he could find, and hurried them towards his white domain through the fields of corpses. He kicked the door open and let them all run inside before him. He pushed them into the first door on the left, which looked like a large, blank, white hall. Nothing was in there but floor space, and plenty of it. "Wait here," he said to them all.

Lucifer rushed out of the room, and ran into the room at the end of the hallway. He stopped quickly as he set foot in the room, and looked up at his throne. There was somebody sitting in it. Somebody who looked very familiar, but not quite. He thought it was Marcus for a second, but the hair was short and black, not long, brown, and wavy. He stood back with the look of confusion in his eyes. "Lucas?" he asked.

Lucas instantly disappeared, and Lucifer ran back to the room with all of the damned humans. He stood at the end and shouted to them all. "This is the end, I'm afraid. You have all been sent here for one of two reasons. One, you were wicked enough to warrant being sent to Hell. Or two, you just didn't know any better. Those of you who fall into the second category, this is your lucky day. You have been granted a second chance. So, goodbye!" he said.

Half of the people in the room disappeared. Lucifer looked at the rest of them. "As for the rest of you, enjoy your stay!" He rushed out of the room, and out onto the street. He flew towards where Marcus and Ben were still battling demons. He pulled his sword and began cutting through them to reach Marcus and Ben. The three of them formed a small triangle, facing away from each other. The demons all stayed back, but the army of angels came behind them from all directions, and swung their swords until there were no more demons standing between them and Marcus, Ben and Lucifer. Marcus raised his sword in the air, and the army of angels did the same. They all cheered, and Ben and Lucifer joined in.

"So, now I'm left with Hell and all these people, and no one to help me punish them," Lucifer said, as Marcus and Ben were getting ready to leave.

"You won't be alone," Marcus said. "Some angels will stay behind to help you, and you might even get some of the people to change their ways and help you."

"Just come and get me if you need me, okay?" Lucifer asked.

"Without a doubt," Marcus said. "Thanks."

Marcus put his hand on Lucifer's' shoulder. "Take care, brother," he said.

Marcus and Ben turned to walk out the entrance. "And Ben," Lucifer called out. Ben turned around. "Don't be a stranger, now."

Ben smiled. He turned back towards the entrance and walked back to Earth with Marcus. They found themselves standing at the foot of Devils' Tower. Marcus grabbed Ben on the shoulder, and they were instantly back at Ben's house. The floor was still dirty and the window was still smashed. "I forgot about all of this. How am I supposed to fix all this?" Ben asked.

Marcus smiled. "Check your bank balance," he said.

Marcus turned to walk out the front door. "Wait, where are you going?" Ben asked.

Marcus looked up at the ceiling. "I'm going home," he said. "I figure you've got this place covered. I'll see you soon."

"Marcus, wait," Ben said. "I never got the chance to thank you. You've really been there for me, and I'm thrilled to be a part of this with you."

"Don't mention it," Marcus said.

"Hey Marcus?" Ben asked.

"Yeah?"

"Where exactly is Heaven?" he asked. "I mean, I know it's at the top of Devils' Tower, but where exactly is it?"

"You mean after all this, you still need me to tell you that?" Marcus asked.

"Well, yeah," Ben said.

Marcus tapped his own chest with two curled fingers. "In here," he said.

Marcus walked out the door and disappeared. Ben sat down on the couch and stared at the floor. He reached beside the couch, and pulled out a laptop computer bag. He unzipped it and pulled out his Compaq laptop computer. He started it up and sat it down on the couch. He walked to the fridge and pulled out a beer. He opened the second drawer in his kitchen and pulled out a bottle opener and popped the cap off the bottle, then put the bottle opener back in the drawer and pulled out a soft packet of cigarettes. He pulled out one of the cigarettes and lit it with a lighter he kept near the stove, then left the packet of cigarettes on the kitchen bench. He walked back to the couch and sat down next to the laptop. He put his beer on the table next to the couch, and put the computer on his lap. He opened up a word processor and began to type his thoughts.

Sunday, 4ᵗʰ May, 2008

I'm only twenty-four, and I hadn't seen all that much. I guess I have been quite naïve about the world. I met Marcus when I was a teenager, and he showed me a world I hadn't seen. He taught me all about fighting, and made me read the bible, as crass as that seems with his demeanor, and I never really saw that he knew exactly what he was talking about. Until now.

After seeing Heaven and Hell, and becoming an angel, I have seen what this world could become. I don't know how much influence I could have on this place. I guess, when it comes down to it, Marcus gave me the one thing that so many people promise to someone else, but they never deliver. He gave me the world. And I'll do what I can with it. I have seen that evil can become good, just as good can become evil. I have gained a new friend with which I thought was the epitome of all evil. But inside, beats the heart of a young boy.

I have seen strength beyond my imagination, and I still can't believe that after all this time, my best friend is an angel. And better yet, now, so am I. The inspiration I have gained from the past few days has given me so much, that I feel like writing about it. Writing journals, like Marcus has. I never even knew he wrote journals. I'd love to read them someday, if he'd ever let me. And, what is this

Downfall? He's told me so much these past few days, and yet there's still so much I don't know about him. I'm sure he'll tell me in time.

So, in the meantime, I'll just write my own thoughts down. Maybe even try to get published or something. I don't know if that will go anywhere, but it's worth a shot. Maybe it'll help me teach the people of Earth the truth, and maybe I could show them what living is all about. I have lived, and now I can live knowing that wherever I go, I will always have a guardian angel watching over me. I don't know when, or if I will see Marcus again. But I hope to God, that it will be someday soon.

Ben saved the file and closed his laptop, and put it back down beside the couch. He decided to relax and watch a bit of television to let himself unwind. He'd had a big few days, and even though his house looked like a bombsite, he didn't have the motivation in him to clean it. Eventually, he went and found a tarp and some tape, and began to cover up the window to keep the draft out. After that, he grabbed his cigarettes off the kitchen bench and put them in his breast jacket pocket, as he headed for the front door. He walked out the front door and closed it behind him, and walked down the street.

The sky was dark and covered with stars. He looked up and imagined Heaven in his head. He turned right at the end of his street, and walked the familiar way to Murphy's. The streetlights lit up the buildings all around an eerie yellow, as he continued walking. He wasn't quite sure why he was heading to Murphy's. Maybe it was just instinctual, or maybe he felt Marcus would be there. He stepped down an alleyway in between some tall buildings, and a hooded figure turned in behind him. It kept its distance as it followed, whilst he used the alleys as shortcuts. The figure continued to follow him as he walked, with no idea of what was about to happen next. But, Marcus stood on a rooftop above with his sword in his hand, and looked down at Ben being followed. He watched closely as he knew what was about to happen. "It's going to be a little sooner than you would think, my friend," he said.

To be continued...

About the Author

Beginning a lifetime of music at the young age of four, singing for family and friends, Matt found he had caught the music bug. He furthered his talents, first learning to play the guitar at the age of eight. Matt formed many bands over the years, playing in many venues across Victoria and interstate.

After the death of his brother in 2005, Matt took a large break from playing gigs and began writing his first novel, Sword of the Angels. The story quickly developed into a trilogy, which gave him an outlet for his grief; allowing him to create characters and situations for the memory of his brother to live on.

The Revelation Trilogy is a fictional novel about the struggle of balance between good and evil, with friendship, adventure, betrayal, war, and unlikely alliances.

www.whitelightpublishing.com.au

www.ingramcontent.com/pod-product-compliance
Lightning Source LLC
Chambersburg PA
CBHW070011120726
47909CB00003B/880